Cloned for Reward, Call to Duty

Stephen Lewis

Introduction

Steven Lewis was a shell of a man, heart broken by a bitter divorce and the loss of his children. His life wasn't what he'd always thought it would be. Even, his job was letting him down. He felt defeated by circumstance, and he eventually found solace in the bottle. Drinking became the one thing that made him forget the world around him. He lived day by day, unaware that his past was about to collide with his future.

One chance meeting with old friends changes his life forever. They remember the military man he used to be – strong, determined, a brother you could count on. They had an opportunity for him, one that he couldn't refuse. This chance meeting was his *Call to Duty*.

This is his story. The story of how his life took a drastic turn, a turn for the better. His ultimate mission will unfold before your eyes with unbelievable events that will have you asking if any of it could possibly be true. (It is) The Lambs of God's cult will leave you haunted with visions of torture and destruction. The twists and turns will leave you at the edge of your seat. Will Steve have what it takes to save Susannah from these vicious people? Did he make the right decision going back to duty?

CLONED FOR REWARD
CALL to DUTY

Susannah Kavanagh was no ordinary teenager, living with her loving caring grandparents in a 17th century stately home in Scotland, not far from the beautiful city of Edinburgh. The Kavanagh family could trace their ancestors right back to the construction of Kavanagh house was built in 1645 by Alistair Kavanagh, who was a commander in the English civil war. He had been given titles and land in bony Scotland for services rendered to the crown. The family, thanks to Cromwell, fled to Scotland severing all ties with England.

The Kavanagh family are and always have been well liked, respected, and greatly involved in their surrounding community. At the young age of only seventeen, Susannah was turning out to be a fine young lady. This was pretty remarkable due to her losing her parents in a light air craft accident 18 months earlier.

Susannah had approximately a year to go before inheriting the family fortune of millions and the responsibility which came with the Kavanagh name.

Whilst Susannah and her Grandparents looked forward to a bright future, unbeknown to them, an evil presence Harold Fletchly the leader of a religious cult called Lambs of God, had different plans for Susannah. Without any family members even suspecting anything untoward was going on, the grooming had started. Plans which had been in the making for years were now active and gaining great momentum.

Fletchly was not concerned with the family's millions. He wanted the priceless prize of the Kavanagh name and lineage. He wanted to become a member of the British elite would make is plans so much easier. In his evil and twisted genius mind, he was already a Kavanagh.

Stephen Lewis was an ex-soldier who had just been through one hell of a messy divorce. He was about as low as you could get, when luckily for him, he accidentally bumped into a couple of friends from at least ten years ago when Steve was serving in the Army. Within weeks of this chance meeting, Steve found himself working for a government department that doesn't exist. He left his 9-5 and became a member of the world we all just read about or watch on TV... He'd been CALLED to Duty.

My Life

MONDAY TO FRIDAY I work on building sites as a scaffolder. Not the greatest job in the world, especially in the winter months when the steel tubes glue themselves to the skin on your hands. Not to mention… the pay is shit. Twelve months ago, I split from my partner and two kids, which seems to be a very common occurrence these days. After ten years living with someone, tucking your kids in every night then all of a sudden, your life is a roller coaster. I went from being a loving, full time dad, to being suddenly tossed into a new roll of part time father. With limited access to my two children, not to mention the limited funds (*Child Support Agency*), it seems you need to spend more money on your children, even when you're spending time with them.

Anyone who's been through a relationship break-down knows about the emotional turmoil it causes. Basically, my head was in bits, and my body was starting to follow. This was unlike me. I've always tried to keep myself in good shape as a rule. That was before the drinking. Don't get me wrong… I've always enjoyed a drink, but this was as if I couldn't stop myself. I seemed to need the beer to switch off… not good. It was also starting to affect my work, but I kept on turning to drink. I was in debt. My wages were not enough to cover my outgoings, after the ex-had pilfered more than half of it. Even so, I still continued to spend whatever money I had left over on drink.

Every night, whilst shopping at the local supermarket, it was as if I had blinkers on. As soon as I walked through the automatic sliding doors, I took the same route to the beer shelf... the same time... every night. The only thing that changed was whether or not I added Cider to my list. It just depended on how low I felt. What did they think of me at the checkouts? Piss head probably. And, who could blame them? They couldn't see the pain inside; they only saw the outside shell. (And it was starting to crack)

This particular night, I had been working late doing some over time on site and because of this, my habitual instinct for my comfort blanket had gone to pot. I tried my best to look inconspicuous, which is hard to accomplish when you're over six feet tall, eighteen stone, and unshaven with a baseball cap on backwards.

Just then a male voice said, "Is that you Steve?"

I turned slowly to the sound of the familiar, yet unnerving voice, to be faced with a blast from the past... Chris Johnson, a good friend from my Army days. It had been a good ten years since I'd last seen him.

I said, "You haven't changed, Chris."

He replied, "You have mate. You look like a zombie!"

"Nice to see you, too," was my sarcastic response, but I was self-consciously aware that he was right.

I turned to grab my fix off the shelf. Whilst talking to Chris, I heard another familiar voice saying "Who's paying for all this food Chris? It should be on expenses."

At that point Basher popped his ugly head from around the back of the cider bottles. It was a real breath of fresh air to see Basher and his ginger hair. He looked exactly the same as he had ten years ago. Bash was stumped for words when he saw me. Getting over the initial shock, we talked about old times as we made our way to the checkouts. The tills were all busy except for the Baskets Only line. I walked up to pay, and I could see the checkout girl's eyes staring like saucers, behind me. I turned to see Chris and Bash carrying their trolley as if it was a basket. It had been a long time since I had laughed, really laughed. Once outside, I started to say my goodbyes when Chris asked if I needed a lift home.

I told him, "I only live around the corner."

"Get in the car anyway," said Chris.

I found myself walking to the car with him and Bash. Nice car as well, one of the new Audi's. Chris probably fancied himself as Steve McQueen. The doors opened impressively with one of those remote control gadgets. We were sitting at the junction waiting to pull out of the car park, when Chris pressed a button on the dash. What I thought was the front of the ash tray, turned around and a little screen lit up. A voice, sounding like something out of Star Trek, prompted, *'no messages please log on'*. I was that stunned by the little voice and screen, I realized too late we were passing my drive.

"Stop!" I shouted.

Chris then slammed on the brakes, pulled over and reversed back to my drive. Basher, just as forward as I remembered, invited himself and Chris in. *Well*! When we went through the back door and into my kitchen, suddenly for the first time in months it hit me... and hit me fucking hard. The place had, unnoticed by me, transformed into a pig sty. The sink looked like it was breeding dirty pots. We'd lived together in Barracks and even holes in the ground which were more hygienic than my kitchen.

We made our way through to the lounge and sat on furniture, which would have probably looked more at home in a squat. Chris looked at me in a way which said he was thinking of a hundred questions at once. He gave a glance that made me see the dozens of empty beer cans scattered around the room for the first time.

Chris then said, "What the fuck as happened to you Steve?"

How could I even begin to answer his question? This man was someone who had known a totally different me.

Bash, bless him, at this point had gone back into the kitchen and shouted "Have you any bin bags, Steve?"

He had begun making himself busy clearing up. I didn't know whether to stop him and say I would do it later. I just did not know what to say to either of them. I felt empty, tired and disgusted with myself. At the same time though, I was really pleased to have seen them both.

I sat down. My head now in my hands. I was exhausted. "I'm sorry, Chris. I'm a failure," I mumbled.

I could hear Bash asking if I had any tea or coffee. Chris told him to get the brew kit out of the car. I heard him come out of the kitchen, walking across the bare wooden floors and pass through the living room, but I didn't have the pride left to pick my head out of my hands to look at him. Chris stood up, tapped me on the shoulder a few times and then left after Bash. I now felt even more ashamed of myself. I had managed to disgust two of my old, true and good friends.

Then, I heard the door and creaking floors as they came back in. Bash went through to the kitchen asking as he passed "Do you take sugar Steve?"

Chris stood in front of me saying, "Where do you want to put this lot?"

I looked up through tear soaked eyes, and Chris was stood there with all the groceries they'd just bought. Once the food was put away, Basher brought our brews through and they both sat down.

Bash asked, "Are you working?"

Before I could answer Chris continued the questions, "Where is your family? What has happened to your house?"

That was my cue. It all came out, for what seemed like hours. I talked and they just listened, apart from when I grabbed for one of my cans. Bash took it from me. He poured it, along with the rest of the cans, down the sink which was now empty of dirty dishes thanks to him washing up.

It was around 1:00 a.m. when Chris said it was time for them to be getting back to their digs.

I said, "You might as well stay the night."

Bash, already half asleep, turned to Chris, "We might as well. We've got an early morning brief at BP and it's just up the road". They were stopping in digs because as far as I remembered, Basher was from Leeds and Chris was from Bradford.

It was Friday night or I suppose early hours of Saturday and I didn't have to go to work that morning. Yet, for the first time in months I had gone to bed without having a drink.

I arose around 10:00 a.m. Chris and Bash had already left. I think I would have believed I'd dreamed the whole episode if it was not for the kitchen. I just smiled to myself, it was so clean.

"Thanks, Bash," I thought to myself.

THE NEW BEGINNING

16.00 Hours Saturday

THERE WAS A knock on the front door. I came through from the kitchen and the first thing in my vision was Basher's face squashed up against one of the Georgian window panes in my lounge bay. A frightful sight for those that didn't know him!

I opened the door with energy, and Chris walked in saying, "Any chance of a brew, Steve? We've just spent four hours breathing in some shitty chemicals at BP."

They were working for another of our mates, Dave Sissons, as security advisers, and they had just completed a four hour rekey at BP. They would be going back at a later date to set up and carry out an O.P. (Observation Point) due to possible sabotage at the plant. Dave Sissons was also from Bradford and probably the 'hardest' man I have ever known. He was a good man to have on your side when in a spot of trouble.

The last time I had clapped eyes on Dave was when I was demobbed (approx. ten years). He was in the Camp Cells, Glass House. I had loaned him £50, and he told me he was going AWOL to America. He had made some contacts over there on our last posting. Chris then went on to say, he was doing very well for himself with his security and personal protection company. My mind went years back to our American tour, eight weeks in Fort Lewis. (A really good time.) Apart from one day with Chris but that's another story.

Chris then brought me round from my thoughts, "Do you have a car and some decent clothes?"

"I have a car, but it's not a lot of use without Insurance or Road Tax." I replied.

When it came to clothes, well I had a couple of pairs of tatty jeans, a lumbar jacket with paint on it and a suit, shirt and stuff from my days as a Scaffolding Manager. The days before my family had fractured and split apart.

Bash, elbowing Chris, said "Go on, tell him what Dave said."

Chris reaching for his wallet pulled out and handed me a £50 note. "Dave says he owes you that, and here's another couple of hundred from Bash and me."

"I can't take that! I don't know when I could pay you back," I replied.

"Give it back when you're back on your feet again," replied Bash forcing the notes into my hand.

Chris continued, "In the meantime, check if your suit fits, get it cleaned and pressed for next Thursday night."

"What the fuck you on about Chris?" I couldn't take it all in, two of the best mates I have had, stood in my now clean kitchen like angels reigniting my life.

"We've got you some part-time work through Dave. We told him you were a bit down on your luck and short of cash."

At that point Bash butted in saying, "Don't worry, Steve. We haven't mentioned your drinking and won't if you lay-off it. You don't need that shit, Steve. Get some adrenalin back in your system that will sort you out."

My head was spinning. For the first time in months, I felt like a person with a life again and not just someone putting a brave face on when he saw his kids and borrowing money to take them out. Not really knowing what to expect from this job, I asked Chris what I'd be doing.

Chris wrote down a telephone number, "Ring this on Thursday lunch time and don't make plans for that night."

"What are you getting me into?" I kept saying.

"Don't worry. He'll start you off light. Anyway, we've got to get going. We've got a lot on."

Shaking hands and a good slap on the back off Bash telling me how great it was to see me again. We said our goodbyes, and they had gone as quickly as they had appeared.

———————

Both Monday and Tuesday came and went, and I was actually keeping sober for once. Wednesday night around tea time, I picked up my kids. My son and daughter's little faces lit up when I arrived and bibbed the car horn.

My very own angel, my daughter, then said, "You

look happy, dad." She then kissed me saying, "Big squeeze!"

My son then asked if we were going for a meal (probably because I was in the car.)

I told him, "Yes, if you want to."

We arrived at Paull, a small village just outside Hull, East Yorkshire and parked up the car. Both of them sprung out of the vehicle like Labrador puppies. They had so much energy. I remember thinking the last couple of times they had been with me they had been quiet but they were the total opposite today.

It's amazing that you and your emotions are such a catalyst to their feelings. Within thirty seconds of their launch from the car, they were on the beach. Lewis in a rock pool, and Abigail was tormenting the surf as it broke on the shore. I felt really proud. I joined Abigail at the shore line, and we tried spinning flat stones, seeing how many times they bounced before sinking.

Forty minutes had flown by and I shouted "Come on we have to go and order meals."

It must have been the word 'meals' because they both froze. They glanced my way then at each other as if to indicate *race you*, and then sprinted to me. Grabbing their hands we crossed the road and into the Rose & Crown. A large one story building painted white, aesthetically pleasing to the eye. The kids loved it because attached to the beer garden was a well-stocked children's play area. I loved this place because of the steak. My food came on an oval cast iron plate still sizzling… sorry train of thought went a little then.

11.45 Hours Thursday morning.

I TOLD THE Foreman on site I was going to the fish shop. The pay phone was about a twenty minute walk away. My adrenalin was flowing just with the anticipation of making the call. Not knowing what to expect, I needed to calm myself down. It was a crazy feeling, but it was wonderful, buzzing in your own skin. The phone rang for what seemed like hours, but was actually about thirty seconds. A female voice answered, and I asked to speak to Dave.

She was obviously expecting my call as the next thing she said was, "Is that Steve?"

Surprised I replied, "Yeah."

She went on, "I need you to tell me what date you left the Army?"

I replied, "March 6th, 1994."

"Thank you. I also need you to answer the next question immediately. If not, this conversation will cease."

She then asked me for my Army number. She accepted my answer and said she would put me through.

The next voice, also female, asked me if I was free tonight. On answering yes, she told me to be at the Trust House Forte Hotel on North Ferribey. I was told to enter the car park at 18.00 hours and remain in my vehicle. She thanked me for my co-operation and the line went dead. I was so taken aback. The receiver still at my ear when the recording, "*The other person has cleared. Please replace the handset,*" brought me to my senses.

I'd been expecting to have a chat with Dave and instead it was like something out of the *007* Movies. It didn't matter. I was feeling exhilarated and that was all that counted at that moment, even thought I was still none the wiser at what to expect.

17.45 Hours

THERE I WAS, sitting in my car in the hotel car park, wearing jeans and a t-shirt, my suit in the boot. It would have caused a lot of questions if I had walked out of the plastic portable loos on a building site at work in a suit.

18.00 Hours

ON THE DOT, a car pulled up about five spaces to my right. It was an Audi just like Chris's car, so I guessed this might be my connection. The driver seemed to be having a conversation on a mobile phone. He got out of the car and made his way over to me. He was in his early forties and smart but casually dressed. He was ordinary looking with short hair and slightly above average height and build, in good shape, physique wise. As he got closer to the car, I opened my window.

"Steve?" he asked.

"Yes, I'm Steve."

"I'm Arthur."

I got out of my car and was about to greet him and tell him my suit was in the boot, when he said, "Thank fuck for that. I thought you were going to be another one of those suit boys, thinking you're a spy or something!"

I didn't mention the suit in the boot. Would you? I got into Arthur's car and belted up. As he drove out of the car park and headed onto the motorway, that voice from Star Trek said, "*messages in sequence, please log on to receive.*"

After about ten minutes of silence, I initiated a conversation about the car and the last time I had heard 'the voice from Star Trek.' He gave me a surprised glance and wanted to know when I had seen the other 'clocking on machine', as he called it. I told him I had been in a mate's car and it looked and sounded identical. Arthur told me he hadn't heard of any other company logging on with their system.

"My mates work for Dave," I said.

"You have friends working for Dave? I was told you were a new one to the game… Green as they say. We get a lot of club bouncers starting with us looking to get in to body guarding. The size of you, I took you for one of them… Who are your friends?" asked Arthur with genuine interest.

"Bash and Chris….."

Before I could get Chris's surname from my lips, Arthur jumped in with, "not the joking duo, with enough spirit to get the whole British Army in shit."

I replied, "I think they have a couple of times."

"Were you in the Army with them?" asked Arthur.

"Yes, we were in the same brick in Northern Ireland for 2 years." Now on a new platter with Arthur, I asked "What can I expect to happen tonight?"

"Not much, Steve. It's what we call Airport runs. Really it's just upmarket courier work. Dave uses these sorts of jobs to keep us full timers going between assignments. It's also Dave's way of putting new recruits through an assessment test. But if you've served two years with Chris and Bash, you won't need one. Maybe a shrink," he said jokingly... I think.

"I thought Dave was in the brick as well?" Arthur said as he glanced in his mirrors.

"He was," I said. "He took over after old Mick sort of retired in our second year."

Just then, we cut across from the outside lane doing ninety mph, ending up cruising at fifty mph and indicating for the Bradford turn off. It had all gone quiet in the car, so I took advantage of this. And tried to memorize the route. As the turn off appeared, I felt the cat's eyes under the wheel, making that thudding noise. Arthur adjusted the wheel slightly and the thudding was eliminated. Just after leaving the motor-way, we pulled over into a lay-by.

"Do you want a sandwich and a coffee, Steve?" asked Arthur.

"Yes please." Giving you some indication of how nervous I was. I thought I'd feed the butterflies in my stomach. At the same time I began to wonder about my judgment and asked myself whether or not I was doing the right thing. I wasn't frightened, compared to some of the operations in N. Ireland we had carried out, but that was a fucking long time ago... a different life. A different world.

At that point Arthur returned. The car door opened, and first in was the really nice and instantly recognizable aroma of hot tom and bacon. I was then passed two polystyrene cups of steaming coffee in a light grey pulp paper tray and two paper bags, twisted tight making the tomato juice seep through.

"Bacon and tomato, Steve?"

"Cheers Arthur. What do I owe you?"

"Expenses mate. Normally we would get something to eat on the plane but I don't know if we will be flying out or just collecting."

"Flying! I'm at work tomorrow morning at 8.00am," I said, nearly choking on my sandwich.

"How much do you get a day Steve?"

"About £80 after tax," I replied.

"Well, if we do fly, you'll get £240 clear and £20 cash for petrol. If we pick up at the airport, you will get £120 clear plus petrol money and even if we fly, you will still be back at your car for around 04.00 hours," explained Arthur.

This put one of those happy little smirks on my face, the one's you try not to show but feel. After all, I was well and truly skint. (Penniless)

19.45 Hours

WE PULLED UP outside a taxi office in a part of Bradford you really wouldn't want to slow down in, let alone stop.

Arthur got out of the Audi to enter the taxi office,

"I won't be long, keep an eye on the car mate." He

said slamming the door then looked right and left and ran across the road.

The office was situated within a row of nine shops. It had a virtually all glass shop front with a three by three feet sign displayed. The windows resembled smoked or tinted glass because of the build-up of dirt. The sign read in big red letters '*Runners in Wanted.*' Next to this sign was a smaller one which read '*one bed flat above for let.*' The only other property to be occupied was an off licence/ mini market.

I could make out a gentleman wearing a turban stood on the other side of the window near a till. He was moving things around biding time, waiting for the illusive customer to appear. All the remaining buildings in this forgotten row were so dilapidated. You would have expected a bull dozer to come around the corner at any time to complete the demolition. I then found myself reading a flyer, offering free needle exchanges and counselling for alcohol issues which had been pasted to a sheet of ply wood that had been used crudely to board up one of the derelict windows.

When Arthur arrived back he was carrying what looked like a small, steel briefcase. He got in the car, closing the car door behind him and locked it. "Give us your wrist Steve?"

As I put my left arm over to him, he commented "The size of you, they've less chance getting this away". He meant the briefcase, as it was handcuffed to my wrist. "Not too tight Steve, I hope? It won't be coming off for a couple of hours. We're flying," Arthur said, as if I understood everything.

Just then, what with the state of the area where we had picked up the case, the fact that it was attached to my wrist and we were heading to an airport, all I could think about was drugs! (*Slight panic attack*.) What was I getting into? I asked myself again.

We pulled out of the street, and Arthur shifted up a couple of gears. Then, he started to push numbers into his clocking on machine, which replied "Hello number 1870", in a very sexy computerised voice.

Arthur replied, "1870 logging on. Pick up 19.55 hours. Flight 20.40 hours. Document class 'C'."

The computer replied, "1870 logged on."

Arthur came back with, "Also log on number 3286, same details. Terminate message."

"We'll be at the airport in about 20 minutes, Steve," Arthur said as we drove by four working girls trying to wave us down, all of them wearing mini-skirts that would pass well as belts.

"That was a nice neighbourhood," I mentioned to Arthur.

He replied, "Perfect cover, Steve. Perfect cover," as he slowed down to navigate the roundabout. 2nd left he indicated then foot down and I felt the G force sit me back in my chair. The next 20 minutes seemed a long time, worrying that I might be carrying a briefcase full of what might be some type of contraband.

As we entered the short stay car park at the airport and came to a halt, I had to say something, "Look Arthur, I'm not being funny, but how do I know I'm not being used as a Mule to carry drugs?"

"At last," Arthur replied. "I wondered when you would ask that. I had you down as someone who thinks and not just follows. Don't worry, Steve. As soon as we enter the airport, we'll pick up our tickets and then we go through to a private room with two custom officers. They'll sign and check our case. Then the same will happen on the other side in Amsterdam. Let's get our tickets, and then we will have time to grab a quick coffee."

Arthur's response eased my mind of 90% of my doubt. As we entered the airport I could feel my adrenalin starting to flow again. I was trying to be professional and cool, especially in front of the Air Hostess giving us our tickets. After we left the ticket desk, we walked towards the stairs, leading to the lounge. The foyer was pretty empty approximately forty-five passengers and then a few cleaners. The front one was picking up litter and tipping the bins into her trolley. The second was a man with a powered floor buffer polishing the already ridiculously shinny floor.

Arthur then spotted two men, and went over and started talking. They were very smartly dressed with black suits on and prominent ear pieces. They both stood facing Arthur in a semi-rigid pose with their arms and hands forming a relaxed triangle shape downwards. The sort of Kevin Costner, bodyguard type of image.

Arthur introduced me and just as I was shaking the second man's hand, he turned to his partner and said, "Let's go. Our pickup is here." (The client)

Arthur and I then had to go straight through to the check-in and just like he had said, went through to a private room.

20.40 Hours

BOOKING IN, I felt one hundred percent about the briefcase. We went into the room with the Custom Officers. I had to put the briefcase on a desk. There were two officers, one of them stood directly in front of me, and the other officer was standing across the table, chatting with Arthur and removing papers from the steel case. The whole process must have lasted five to six minutes, but this removed a mass of doubt from my head. The only thing required of me whilst in the room was to sign a declaration form stating the date, time, and the document numbers of the papers that I was carrying.

Arthur had signed just above me, declaring he was the authorised inspector of the documents. We left the room and Arthur enquired if I was okay, in a way which implied he had concerns for the anxieties I was going through.

I smiled and nodded slightly and then replied "Sure, thanks mate."

We proceeded to make our way to the Boing Airplane and then the seats assigned to us. The Air Hostess started talking softly to Arthur. I was beginning to imagine both the pilot and the co-pilot coming down to see him next. After all, he was even on first name terms with the two Customs Officers. Then, there were the two men in black characters that could have been straight out of a J Edgar Hoover movie. Finally, as we sat down, Arthur sat in the seat near the aisle and I sat near to the window. The seat in between us was left vacant. I found out later we had booked that seat as well. It did come in handy for the brief case.

After watching the gorgeous air hostess complete her little safety routine, which I found quite nice to watch, we got the '*safety belt on*' sign. The Hostess then walked up and down the plane, pushing shut the overhead luggage compartments whilst checking belts were on. The frightening and exciting sounds of the massive Rolls Royce engines warming up as we taxied before the take-off, then the almighty roar as the engines were thrust to full power.

21.10 Hours

WHEN THE '*Seat belt off*' sign appeared, Arthur turned and said, "Steve, if you want to go to the toilet, I need to check the cubicle first and then I will wait outside for you".

I asked "What if you need to go?"

"That will be the only time I remove the case from your wrist and wear it, and then you take my role," Arthur finished.

"Our roles Arthur? What are they? I'll come clean with you. I haven't got a clue what I am doing or what we are doing."

"I thought you'd got into this via Chris and Bash?" he asked.

"Yes I did" I answered.

Arthur came back with "Didn't they fill you in on a few things?"

"Nope, I'm totally in the dark. That's why I was a bit jumpy about the briefcase and going through the airport," I explained.

Arthur said, "My fault then. Right, I'll start from the beginning. The briefcases we pick up and deliver are split down into categories. Remember when I logged on and told the computer document Class 'C'?"

"Yes," I replied.

"Well, basically there are 4 categories: *A, B, C*, and *D*. *A* and *B* have to be escorted by two persons, *C* can be escorted by one or two persons. Judged by the people in the office, *D* is always escorted by one."

Enthralled with what Arthur was saying I asked, "What determines the category then?"

Sharply Arthur said, "That's a question you don't ask. You will find out if you need to know. There are certain things in this job you can get away with. However, the most important rule to remember is confidentiality and trust. Basically trust the people you're working with and trust nobody else and make sure you can trust them, any doubts don't trust."

I didn't know it at this time, but this was the beginning of a solid relationship between Arthur and me, which would bring out more than trust.

"If you get the opportunity to do some assignments with us you'll get a much better picture of what I mean regarding trust? You however, with your background, should have a bloody good idea already."

Arthur gave me a look for me to confirm his words. I nodded in compliance that he was right, and he was spot on with what he had said. I had been in enough scrapes to realize this. Just then, the gorgeous air hostess arrived with the trolley.

"Would you like a drink Arthur?"

"Yes, coffee please Sue." Casually responded Arthur, "Do you want anything, Steve?"

"Coffee for me please" I replied, not taking my eyes off Sue.

As she passed our drinks over she said, "If you would like anything else, please call."

I wondered if she would have said that if she knew what I had in mind. Then she was gone and Arthur brought me back to earth saying "dream on!"

After my reality check, I continued to squeeze information out of Arthur. "So who were those two guys in suits you were chatting to in the Airport?"

Arthur replied, "Two American Close Protection Officers or CPO's. Bodyguards basically, if you are not familiar with this field. However the term bodyguards should only be used if you are not in this field."

During the aeroplane journey I discovered that Dave's security company was made up of two main sections, which were Close Protection and Surveillance. Yet, Arthur mentioned a couple of odd situations which got me thinking there was more to the company. I got the distinct feeling Arthur wasn't telling me everything and that the surveillance section was not just watching people.

Arthur, I also discovered, had been in the Close Protection industry for around twenty years. He was born and bred not far from Hull, in a small town called Withernsea. His family were all generation farmers, yet Arthur one day pissed off to London, and that's how he got into the close protection work. He had built up over a few years a very good reputation for himself, working for the top business elite in London. However, I'm not sure if you remember a certain very rich newspaper/ media company owner that fell off his boat during controversy of his companies pensions? Well, let's just say after that, Arthur needed a new client and somehow he ended up doing stuff for Dave who had really just got started in the industry.

Dave it seems, had around fifteen to twenty personnel working for him at present, all over the world. Arthur went on speaking, and it became apparent that he was very close to Dave. He was well liked and was very trusted by him, to say the least. After being with the company for seven years, he had built up a very good relationship with not only Dave, but the key members of Delta Security Services. Arthur had this overwhelming self-confidence (not overpowering or bullying). A type of personal quality which is hard to explain. To look at him, you wouldn't instantly label him as a bodyguard or a hard man, but there was something there, something reassuring and genuine.

Arthur then seemed to start talking to himself, yet aiming these statements at me. "There is one question on my mind."

"What's that?" I replied.

"Remember when we logged on in the car and I categorised the documents as C?" asked Arthur.

"Yes" I said, puzzled.

"Well basically… I can't remember the last time I had someone accompany me on a Class 'C' job. Dave must have something going on in his head," said Arthur with curiosity.

"If it helps, Dave knows I'm skint," I added.

"It's more than that. He's got something else up his sleeve. For a start, if you were all together in the army, he's probably trying to get you back into a team with the duo Bash and Chris," Arthur through out there.

"No. I'm just after a bit of extra cash to catch up with a few debts. I've been out of this scene too long," I replied swiftly!

"If Dave has half the trust in you, which he has in Bash and Chris, he will want you working for him. The four of you must have gone through some special and tough times to get such a bond? He's *calling you back to Duty*!" Arthur insisted.

NORTHERN IRELAND

June 1986 Bessbroke

BESSBROKE MILL WAS an old stone cloth manufacturing mill. It had 2-3 foot solid stone walls which were perfect for its new life as a military base, and I mean Military Base. Just about every unit part of or attached to the armed forces had a presence in the mill. The most important attachment to Bessbroke was a group of Indian men. There were around six or seven of them who ran small burger bars, laundries, and tailor services. If you had been out thirty-six to forty hours on patrol, with no sleep and not much to eat if anything, the best sight to see would be a Mucker G hanging around the sleeping rooms, waiting for the bricks burger and laundry order. You would get your food back in around 40 minutes and your uniform in about 4-6 hours. It came back repaired, washed, pressed and at a cost of £3-£10, depending on the repairs.

They also sold this fabric spray for your bullet proof vest, which after a long patrol would stink like a tomcat's piss – that's the vest not the spray. The vest was better known as 'flak jacket' or 'Kevlar'. It weighs around 10-12 pounds. Basically a stone, and you wore them under your jacket with just a t-shirt under the vest. The vest itself covered the whole torso and was constructed of thousands of nylon fibres woven together with the zip situated on the side plus flaps with Velcro for extra security. This would protect you from a shotgun or possibly a certain type of hand gun fired from a distance.

The real protection of the vest came from two Kevlar plates placed in pockets at the front and the rear of the jacket. These plates covered the vital organs and were able to withstand much more velocity from a shot than the vest itself. After running around the streets of this troubled place with one of those things on, especially in the summer, you can imagine the amount of sweat you would expire, hence the need to purchase the spray. (Sorry, memories flooding back.)

06.10 Hours Tuesday.

WE HAD ARRIVED from Newry in a covert van. A white tatty transit with some made-up carpet fitter's name advertised on the side. The van may have looked like it would have struggled to travel the fifty mile journey we had just undertaken along the back roads of Northern Ireland, with one of its wings virtually hanging off and the front bumper missing. Believe me though, that van was mechanically sound, and its engine more geared up than a national rally car. The driver would also be on par with a lot of rally drivers. There were eight of us in the van plus the driver and his co-driver.

Two bricks were changing places with another two bricks after a two week stint in Newry, which was long enough in that hell hole. Our regiment had been the first British Soldiers back on the street for ten years, and we were not made to feel welcome, if you understand what I mean? The decision to put the army back on the streets of Newry, was made a few weeks earlier after a terrorist had dressed up as a Butcher and walked up to an RUC (Royal Ulster Constabulary) car with four police officers inside. Being August, it was hot, so the doors were open since it was not possible to open the windows of the police cars because they were bullet proof and fixed. The man disguised as a butcher in whites and a blue and white striped apron got within a couple of feet of the vehicle, then pulled out a pistol and shot all four in the head. I believe three died instantly and one survived. The man then tossed a grenade into the car, but forgot to remove the pin, so it stayed inert. (*Some small mercy*) So, I am sure you get a good idea of what we was up against.

Dave Sissons had taken command of our brick due to old Mick moving on to a cushy posting back in England. Dave was a totally different character to Mick. Mick was so laid back. After all, he'd been here a few times. Including back in 1972 on 30th January, *Bloody Sunday*, when the shit was really hitting the fan, so to speak. He only had a couple of years left before getting out of the army, so I guess his latest posting would be an introduction back to civil street. Dave, on the other hand, was twenty-six and had been in the army for just three years. Our first impression of him was he wanted to and was going to make a name for himself and accomplish a high rank. Dave didn't talk much about himself but someone who was also in our regiment had grown up with him. He told us that at eighteen Dave had been a bare knuckle fighter for a couple of years in Bradford. Surviving with his fists and quick wits, travelling and living in the community of some travelling people.

After leaving home at the age of fifteen, due to family issues, he put his dad in hospital. After watching him beat up his mam for years, Dave had had enough. Unfortunately his mother sided with the arsehole of a man who used her as a punch bag, and asked Dave to leave the family home. His fighting had been going well with him being coached and looked after by an old gypsy and his wife. The wife thought of Dave as a surrogate son. Dave soon had a name for himself. His reputation had spread far through most of the travellers who had fighting in their communities. Dave would now be getting £3-4000 per fight, usually in gold. Just after Dave's twenty-first birthday, a fight was arranged between Dave and an old pro from Ireland. This match was billed as the fight of the century. Patrick McShane was the old pro. He was 46 and had over 1000 fights to his name, and he had won the last 800. Dave had around 60 under his belt; he had won 50 of these.

On all accounts the fight took place in Ireland, and lasted nearly two hours. Compared to an average fight time of twenty-five to thirty minutes, was some scrap. No breaks, no gloves, no biting but everything else was allowed. We heard it was pure torture on both sides, and the illegal betting grossed over a million pounds.

Dave in the end came out on top. I wasn't actually told the full fight details, but I know the Irish man was buried two days after the fight and Dave was laid up in bed for ten days with a broken arm and lord knows how many stitches. The only thing that I had found out about Dave before the army was he had given most of his £40,000 purse money from the fight to his old coach and then travelled around on his own for a few years before joining up.

Dave's reputation as an outstanding fighter and hard man within the regiment, became known about a year before he took over as our brick commander. When we, that is the regiment, were just getting ready to leave Berlin, Germany and start our two year posting in North Ireland. Four weeks before we left Brook Barracks, Berlin, we had the battalion boxing championships. I personally was not allowed to box due to getting six stitches above my left eye boxing for IJLB (Infantry Junior Leaders Battalion) in Folkestone, Kent. Basher who had been in the battalion a year longer than Chris and I had received a three year ban from boxing for hitting the Ref and head butting his opponent.

Chris on the other hand was totally against the sport and couldn't see the point in it. Anyway, the night in question, which proved Dave's fearful reputation, was a wet, warmish mid-July night. Just about all the regiment was seated around the ring. 'C' Company, that was our company, were level on points with 'A' Company and the next weight to fight was to be the heavyweights, which was to be the last bout of the evening. 'A' Coy's contender and champion was already warming up outside of the ring. He was looking very relaxed, probably due to the fact he had been champion for 4 years, winning all his fights by the way of KO. 'C' Coy's contender was just a brave chap making the weight. As the boxers were being introduced, we could see our Sgt Major come over to where Dave was sitting and started talking to him.

Then Dave started walking towards the changing rooms. The commentator had entered the ring with the microphone and announced there was to be a substitution of boxers for 'C' Coy. The whole regiment was talking about the swap, and it had got back to us that apparently our Sgt Major had found out about Dave's fighting past. After him continuously saying 'no' he didn't want to fight, Sgt Major had threatened to put the whole company on jankers (punishment duties) for the first two months of our Ireland tour.

He would also personally make sure the only thing Dave was in charge of would be the kitchen sink. Our other boxer left the ring. You could see all the blokes who were running betting books were cancelling the last fight, and only expecting the odds at evens.

Chris also had his book out which was a bit odd as all you got off him was, '*I don't like the sport.*'

Chris was also relaying the odds to evens until Bash said, "If they want it let them leave their bets on 'A' Coy."

Chris said to Bash, "We'll be wiped out if 'A' Coy

wins."

Bash replies, "Dave will walk it. No problem."

The tension and atmosphere was now electric… I'm talking national grid. All the RP's (*regimental police*) were put in the isle between us and 'A' Coy. Every chair in the arena was being banged on the floor. Dave was still outside of the ring just standing there, oblivious as to what was going on around him. Most of the shouting was his name. Just then the commentator tried to silence the crowd but with no avail. The RSM got into the ring and brought us to silence, without the mike I may add.

RSM says, "Please, I do appreciate the excitement, but we must ask 'A' Coy if they accept the substitution of boxers."

Just after the RSM's announcement the current 'A' Coy champ, threw his arms up into the air in acceptance. The roar from 'A' Coy was frightening, and I'm sure even the great Mohamed Ali would have turned. Not Dave. We now noticed that he had been gloved up and both the OC and CSM were talking to him. We presumed this was to wish him good luck. Afterwards, we found out from one of the seconds in the corner, the OC, wanted to know if Dave believed he could win.

Dave answered, "No problem, sir."

The OC taken aback slightly, by Dave's very calm and confident answer, asked. "Will it be by points or KO, Private Sissons?"

Dave's reply was, "KO, first round Sir."

The OC came back with, "If you achieve that prediction Private, you will be a Lance Corporal before we arrive in Ireland." The OC continued to praise him and wish him good luck.

Dave interrupted Major Horseford, "I'll win for the company this time on the condition I'm never asked to fight again."

Both the OC and CSM agreed.

"You must have some good reasons to turn all this glory down son," commented the CSM.

Dave replied, "If you'd been through, in this sport as what I have, Sir, it couldn't possibly hold any glory."

Dave turned at that point and walked up the wooden steps to enter the ring. Major Horseford moved closer the CSM and had to lean right over to his ear to be heard, because the sound barrier was being broken by 'C' Coy shouting '*Sissons!*'

The OC commented to the CSM, "He is one cool soldier. Do you think his prediction will come true?"

"Funnily enough, Sir… I do," replied the CSM, knowing full well the OC would be having a wager with the other officers on all fights.

The RSM once again entered the ring. This time with the use of the mike brought all Companies again to a silence and asked the referee to take over. The referee brought both boxers to the centre of the ring, asked the fighters to touch gloves and to keep the fight clean. Even though there was silence from the crowd, we all waited with anticipation for the bell to sound. You could feel the energy put out. Never in the years that followed during the future fights, did I feel the level of energy expressed as in that night.

The fighters returned to their corners, 'A' Coy's champ sat down whilst Dave continued to stand in his, or should I say our corner. On hearing the bell they came out fighting. 'A' Coy flew at Dave, hitting him with everything he had and it looked impressive. You knew then why he had been Champ for four years. Dave was crouching slightly and covering his head with his gloves. He was getting hit from every angle you could think of and with every punch known in boxing… jabs, right hands, upper cuts, cross, combination and even the famous overhead pounding. Blows Rocky Marciano was notorious for. This continuous beating seemed to go on indefinitely. 'C' Coy had quietened, virtually silent except for Bash. I think he wanted to get in and help.

The Major was making gestures with his hands which suggested Dave was going to end up in the nick, if not hospital. Chris and I kept saying to each other 'A' Coy wasn't hurting him, and you could tell the champ was starting to tire. All of a sudden 'A' Coy pulled away, Dave dropped his gloves and stood up straight, not a mark on him, looking totally unconcerned. 'C' Coy's burner was relit and the name 'Sissons!' once again lifted the roof.

With just seconds of the round left, the Champ came in for a second go, his right hand came out, looking like he wanted to decapitate Dave. Dave continued to just stand there, didn't move or flinch.

You wouldn't blame anyone for thinking Dave was feeling suicidal at this point. The Champ's hand came within inches of connection when Dave's left hand shot up on the inside of the right... a deadly oncoming blow. And cruelly, within a split second, his left hand went to the back of the Champ's head. Dave's right hand then came from nowhere. Sickeningly, the two hands simultaneously crushed the Champ's head. Dave let go of him and stood back to watch him fall to his knees the champ bounced slightly on the canvas. He then fell to his left, his mouth projecting out the gum shield and spit infused blood.

The referee was in and counting, "One... and two... and three..."

The Champ was up for eight and the ref wiped '*A*' Coy's gloves down on his own shirt and said "Box!"

Dave drove in with powerful punches to his opponent's head. The ref dived on Dave's arms at the same time as 'A' Coy threw in the towel. The now ex-champ was out cold on the canvas with the Doctor kneeling beside him. Dave strolled to his corner with no emotions showing... least of all joy.

Dave had now been in charge of our brick for around five weeks, having got his first stripe under unusual circumstances. Saying that, he knew all his stuff and was a '*Very clued up cookie*' as the saying goes. When he got his stripe he also got Basher's undying admiration. Bash loved violence.

Basher's background was a lot different to Dave's. He was brought up on a farm, a Game Keepers' son, near York. If you met his parents, Anthony and Sarah, they would paint a picture of Basher as being loving, warm and tender, quiet and well educated. When, according to Basher's Mother, Tony (Basher's real name) at the age of nineteen fell of a tractor and was in a coma for four days.

On re-gaining consciousness, his parents noticed a disturbing change in Basher's personality. One minute being a caring and sensitive son… the next, they didn't know what to expect. Basher had six 'A' Levels and was taking a year out before going to University. There was a talk of a career in Politics. He was at that time also courting a young girl, whose father was a wealthy land owner and local MP. About six weeks after Basher's accident, it was a warm but damp Thursday evening. The night started when Basher had gone for a walk with his Fiancée Vicky, when suddenly returning home earlier than expected at around 9:30 p.m., Bash decided he was going out again. He was going down to the Local Pub, he told his Mother. This in itself was a very unfamiliar event for Basher. He never visited the pub, except for special occasions.

12.30 a.m. Basher's Parents where woken by the noise of shouting and banging. An unusual occurrence, as their nearest neighbours where about half a mile away. Basher's dad leapt out of bed and ran to the bedroom window. The pleasant warm night had turned cold and wet and all that he could see at first was blue flashing lights, distorted by the amount of rain falling and tired eyes. Anthony let go of the curtains and gulping for air he shouted to wife, Sarah, that he thinks there was an ambulance outside.

Together, grabbing their dressing gowns, they ran down the stairs. They were half way across the stone floor of the old hall of the large 17th Century Cottage, when someone started banging hard on the solid oak door. Then, shouting became clear.

Anthony flung the door open and was met with the sight of Basher in handcuffs being held by two Police Officers and a Police Sergeant standing by. The Sergeant and Anthony were good friends having been at school together, and they constantly came into contact during their working hours in their pursuant of poachers and machinery thieves.

The deadly silence caused by the initial shock was broken by Basher who drunkenly said, "Hi, Mum... Dad. I'm alright, these men have given me a lift home."

At that, one of the Officers pushed Bash as if to say, "Shut up. You're in enough trouble."

Bash did not like this and swung his head around and butted the Officer dead centre on the bridge of his nose. Anthony a calm and quiet man normally, lunged forward and hit Bash Square on the chin. Bash was out cold.

"Bring him in please and put him on the couch," he said.

The Sergeant turning to the other much younger officers, (*one of them covering his wound with a loose hand full of Kleenex tissue, given to him by Sarah*), told them he would deal with this for now and they could take the car back and return to the station.

"I'm sure Anthony will give me a lift back when we have gotten to the bottom of a few things."

"Right, Serge," said one of the Officers as they turned to leave.

Sarah then hurriedly returned from the kitchen with a tea towel and gave this to the blood covered police man, and she again apologized for her son's violent behaviour.

"No need, Ma'am," was mumbled from beneath the tissues. She tenderly folded the towel and gentle removed the tissues. After looking at the wound and then placing the towel in place of the Kleenex, she turned to Stewart the Sergeant and suggested that the wound be looked at the local hospital.

"You're right, of course, Sarah. To the hospital first get that dressed men," sternly ordered the sergeant, the officers said nothing else just confirmed by nodding and proceeded to the police car. The large 300 year old door now closed, preventing any more uninvited cold Yorkshire weather over the threshold.

"Coffee, Stewart?" Anthony said, whilst performing a shiver.

"Have you anything stronger?" was his reply as he was removed his hat and uniformed rain Mack. It had virtually drip dried, forming a puddle on the stone flags.

Basher's Mother at this moment was covering Tony up with a couple of blankets as he was now laid on the wicker couch in the hall way. He had a couple of bruises and scratch marks to the face with lots of blood bleaching his clothes. She motherly kissed his forehead.

Stuart watching said, "Don't worry too much, Sarah. It's not his blood."

Trying not to cry, fighting back the tears, Sarah walked towards the kitchen, choked up she managed to get the words out, "I'll put the kettle on," then exited the Hall into the kitchen.

As Stewart was hanging up his wet gear on the wooden doled pegs protruding from the stone wall.

"I've got half a bottle of Bush mill's Whisky in the study, Stuart," said Anthony.

Stewart nodded and said, "Perfect," as his hand placed his cap on top of his Mack.

Entering the study, Anthony flicked the brass switch on the wall which made the bulb flicker on and off a couple of times, clearly displaying the red hot curled element within the sealed glass case. The old bulb tried once more as if tired, but then managed to illuminate the room from semi darkness. Throwing a handful of chopped wood onto red embers which and been left to die down about three hours earlier Anthony pulled out his chair. Both men sat down, with a familiarity of regular discussions having taken place in the past.

Anthony had set up a group consisting of the local land owners and police representatives with the aim being to stamp out poaching and farm machinery theft. Not Joe Blogg's pinching the odd rabbit and bits from the sheds for his tea or beer money, but the type of theft that had become a million pound a year black market turnover.

Stuart sipping his Whisky, looking across the old large oak antique desk at Anthony said, "Your desk is better than most of the land owners."

"Well, when you save the wealthy thousands of pounds, they have a tendency to be grateful. This was a gift when we got them tractors back from the docks last year."

Just then, Sarah came in holding a tray with a coffee pot and cups on it, noticeable were her eyes red now from the drying of tears.

Having joined them, the discussion turned to Bash. "What's got into him?" asked Stewart, then said, "it was only two months ago he set up a National Database of known poachers." Stuart put his milk and sugar into his coffee and stirred slowly.

"That's just it," said Sarah. "Two months ago was before his accident. Since then, as the Doctor warned us, there has been a change in his behaviour. At the time we didn't think a lot of it. We were just glad he was alive."

Stuart trying to reassure Sarah said, "Tonight's incident will be over looked. The fight Tony got himself into was about 50/50 blame, although the other three men did come off worse the officer will get some compensation and a weeks leave."

The evening finished with the Sergeant getting a taxi back to the station and Basher's parents vouching to keep a closer eye on him over the next few weeks.

The next morning Basher showed no signs or recollection of the previous night's antics, so nothing was mentioned. Over the coming weeks and months after trying all the treatments prescribed by several Doctors. To the despair of his parents, Basher's behaviour became worse, unpredictable and more violent. So after a meeting with his Father and a local retired Colonel, Tony was put forward to join the army. Bash, at this time started on some medication, which helped but did not bring the old Tony back.

Moving on to Chris, well I could write a novel if not a series of novels on Chris's escapades. I'm sure if that happened though a few warrants would be issued in his name, and the army would come looking for him for questioning. He is the only person I have heard of who managed to join the army under a false name, his brothers to be exact. Chris said they were identical twins. I was told the change of identity took place at the age of seventeen between Chris and his brother Wayne, or was it the other way around?

Anyway, Chris and a couple of so called mates got into stealing Lorries from the large lorry parks in and around Leeds and Bradford area. Chris used to enter the lorry parks on his own very early hours. He would break into the lorry parks; rekey the vehicle after he made sure the back was full of items that could be sold easily on markets and in pubs. He would then exit the parks, and phone some others who would come in later to steal the lorry after Chris had hotwired it. The others would go in after him and pick up the vehicle about

6:30 a.m. as if they were the regular driver, and no-one would be any wiser until the driver reported the lorry missing.

Chris never got involved in the actual stealing or the fencing of the gear, which were mainly DVD recorders or other small electrical items. A few weeks after the job, he would get a few grand. He had found a way to smuggle the money out to Jamaica where he had a lot of family and connections made from numerous trips. His parents were born there, and Chris wanted more and realized that if you had money in Jamaica, it was a lovely place to be.

One particular November night, it all went drastically wrong. It was pissing down with rain. He had done his part of the job and had made the phone call. This time the voice on the other end of the line didn't ask for details.

Instead he told him, "Forget that job. We know of one another. A large van filled of circuit boards and chips, and not the frying ones. A contact of mine has offered us £100,000.00 to get it. That's £25,000 cash each tonight. What do you think?"

Chris soaked through to the skin, shivering stood in the telephone box. The door held open with the bottom of his foot, because of the stench of piss and stale beer, thought for a few seconds. He thought about how that would give him a total of £50,000.00 in Jamaica, and this time next week he could be out there looking for a warehouse and starting a new life as a Jamaican entrepreneur.

"Come on. We can't do this without you," said the voice, interrupting his thoughts.

Chris had major doubts it all sounded too good to be true. The rain was getting heavier, but as his eyes gazed over the prostitute calling cards stuck up in the box. The images of his new life in Jamaica won through and he said, "Where do we meet?"

"I'll pick you up at 10:45 outside the Hound & Duck Pub. See you then."

Chris replaced the receiver, and took a deep breath of fresh air as he exited the call box. He pulled on his helmet and got onto his motorbike kick started it and shot off. He only had half an hour, and he needed to get home to change before the meeting took place. Still doubtful, the rain beating down against his helmet and visor, he thought about Jamaica and the £25k again, and the doubts soon eased.

22.55 Hours

OUTSIDE THE HOUND & Duck, Chris waited in the rain, continuously glancing at his watch. His accomplice's then pulled up in a white Toyota. Chris ran to the passenger door and got straight in.

"Nice night to be ten minutes late," he mumbled as he was putting on his seat belt. He knew two of the men in the car. The third he'd never seen before… he was wearing a turban. Later he remembered him only as a short guy and very nasty looking. (*Evil*)

They had been driving for nearly an hour, when they pulled up outside a 24 Hour Cash & Carry near

Manchester. John (shifty) the driver, who had known Chris most of his life and who thought 'morals' were some form of weakness. A slimy shit who would con his own mother for a quid, and these were Chris's own words, not mine. What you have to remember, where Chris grow up in Leeds, you had two choices. Chris, believe me, was not always proud of the one he chose.

John switched off the engine and turned to Chris saying, "You go with Abdul, and he'll show you the van. We'll hang around here. Size will keep an eye open outside, and I'll make sure the car is ready for a getaway if we need it."

Forcing himself to get out once again into the cold pouring rain and trying to keep focused on the £25,000.00 he would be getting. Chris followed Abdul to the fence. Size followed, helping Abdul over first and practically throwing Chris over. Chris laughed to himself and thought Size was the right name for his friend.

Chris ran over to Abdul, who had knelt down near to a large co-cola lorry for some cover from any prying eyes. Crouching down next to him, Chris saw that Abdul had a piece of paper in his hand. It had a registration number written on it with what looked like foreign writing.

It was hard to see with the rain belting down and the only light was from a small red pen torch that Abdul was holding. The lorry and secure compound was vast. There must have been in excess of a thousand different vehicles at least, and at one hundred meter intervals were these towering flood lights lighting up the sky line. It resembled aliens from H G Wells '*war of the worlds*,' however the most disturbing thing in the compound Chris thought, was Abdul. He had a nasty feeling about this man. He was frightening, in a way which Chris had never sensed before.

Still half crouching he was shown a picture of a van by this Abdul, who then pointed to a vehicle. Chris now thinking *let's just get this over with* made his way over to what looked like a brand new Mercedes van, the large sprinter type. He was fiddling about with the lock with a couple of magic tools, as he would fondly call them, when all hell broke loose!

One minute his only problem was tackling a new lock and the next spot lights came on all over, and all he could hear was "STOP. ARMED POLICE! STOP WHAT YOU ARE DOING! ARMED POLICE!"

As it registered as to what was happening, two of the biggest Cop's he had ever seen, ran at him shouting, "Put your arms in the air and stand still."

When they reached him, they didn't stop. One of them spun him round and the other smacked him between the shoulder blades. His head turned to a side; it was crushed against the window of the van, blood everywhere from both his nose and lips.

Bright star lights appeared in his eyes, one of the officers after he had finished frisking him, said to the other, "He's clean, now?"

Carrying on with this, the other officer smashed the butt of his rifle into the back of Chris's head. He fell to his knees, and then, he was kicked down flat. He remembered sucking in the shitty water of a puddle where he lay as he tried to get his breath, when he must have lost consciousness.

As the next thing he knew he was waking up in a clinical type cell at some Police Station or other. He was dressed in a pair of white paper overalls with floppy mittens secured to his hands which were bound with plastic cable ties. Chris just laid there on the floor for minutes without moving, trying to digest the surrounding's and belief as to what had happened. (He knew he was in big shit this time) Just then he heard the door's massive steel locks turn and open, Chis turned to look in the sound's direction.

"We have one awake in here, Serge," shouted a very large copper.

Chris just stared in his direction but not at him. (later Chris told me he was genuinely fucking frightened) The sergeant then appeared at the door, both officers then entered the cell the large constable grabbed Chris's legs. The sergeant picked up his shoulders and the pair then tossed him onto the hard seat with in the cell.

"Someone from special branch wants a word with you. You fucking little traitor," mouthed the sergeant.

Chris's eyes filled with terror, when he realized the sergeant said special branch followed by the word traitor. He sat there with the over whelming urge to mess his self, thinking this must have something to do with that Abdul.

Chris was released after forty-eight hours, having been held on a terrorist charge. Apparently, the van had been full of guns and explosives. He was on bail to appear at Court in about three weeks.

A copper said to him as he was leaving, "Make the most of it, cunt. Say you're good byes. You'll be going away for a long time."

19.30 Hours

THAT NIGHT CHRIS walked through his front door to be greeted by, or was it attacked by his Mother. His Parents were very proud people who couldn't abide trouble with the law. Unlike his brother Chris had always been getting into a bit of bother since the age of 10.

"Where have you been for the last two days?" she demanded to know.

"Staying with friends," Chris lied.

His Father trying to calm his Mother told Chris it was time for him to find his own place to live. He offered to give him £500 to get started, but he wanted him out within a week.

After all the commotion had settled later that evening Chris telephoned his brother, who was visiting relatives in Jamaica for a couple of weeks before returning and starting a career in the British Army.

"Nice to hear your voice, even though you've woke me up. You do know the time difference don't you?"

Chris interrupted him saying, "I've done it this

time. I'll be going down for a long time."

His brother, after listening to the full story, just asked him one question. I think he knew the answer but needed to make sure. "Did you know about the arms and explosives before the Police told you?"

"No, I swear it. I was told computer bits." meekly answered Chris

"Right this is what we will do. As you know I'm supposed to be coming back on Wednesday, and then in the army the following Monday," his brother said calmly.

"Yes," Chris replied.

"Well, I'll stay here for a few months and you'll take my place, shave your head and loose about three pounds in body weight, and nobody will be any the wiser. On your first main leave in sixteen weeks' time. Come out here and we'll swap places."

Chris thanking his brother for saving his life, told him about the money and how to get it. Needless to say the change didn't ever take place.

Chris did visit Jamaica on his main leave, but his brother had used his money to set up a bar and restaurant. He was doing well for himself, in fact their parents were thinking of taking early retirement and moving back to Jamaica to help with the business. Chris figured he owed them that much after all the shit he had caused them. His parents did move back there, and they are also very proud now of the way Chris as turned his life around. The bar and restaurant is one hell of a place.

Bessbroke Mill 06.20hrs
Northern Ireland

WE ALL CLIMBED out of the back doors of the van. The first task you always carry out is going to the loading and unloading bays. You would find these at every entry and exit points in the mill. These were bunkers made of concrete blocks filled with sand. They were designed for soldiers to load and unload weapons safely. We were all carrying small arms as well as our rifle.

This was standard practice for our Battalion when being transported in covert vans. We checked and made safe our own rifle. However, the pistols were checked by an NCO, who then took possession of them and whose job it would be to issue them to the Bricks going back to Newry. After the essentials have been completed, we all made our way to the steel fire escape on the outside of the mill, one hundred and forty-four steps. Which would take us up to our 'lovely' penthouse for the next six weeks.

After two to three days patrol, climbing these steps carrying a two hundred pound Bergen and your rifle, you would be cursing the MOD for not installing a lift. Once in the building you had to hand your weapons in to specially designed armoires situated on all floors of the mill. It would have been usually Bash or I, or both of us who would hand our Brick's weapons in.

Dave normally had a briefing to attend and Chris would just disappear, but would return with food or extra rations of some sort, so none of us ever complained. The mill was a maze of rooms and corridors leading every were and no were, the inside of the 18th century stone mill had everything soldiers would need, except day light, strange feeling,

After a workout in the gym, we would shower and go down for breakfast.

Breakfast in the mill was as good as you would get anywhere in the world. In fact every meal in the Mill was a pleasure. After breakfast, Dave had a briefing to attend, and I would have to get and sign for the morphine, which I carried being the Bricks Medic. I would also be updated on any different medical procedures, and the latest practices which might be needed to be carried out in the field. Whilst this was going on, Bash and Chris would have drawn our weapons out to clean and check, which I would help with on returning.

When Dave turned up, our Brick would have its own briefing to find out what our duties were over the next couple of days. As a rule you would always start on patrol for three or four days, and then work your way through the reaction duties from twenty-four hours standby to two hours standby. Finishing with a twenty-four hour stint on QRF (Quick Reaction Force) which was based on the Heli pad, and your brick never moved of the helipad, unless called to Duty. Then within two minutes, you had to be dressed, awake, armed, and strapped in the helicopter.

It was no different on this occasion except we were lucky, as the time now being 11:10 a.m. Our first patrol was not scheduled until 04.45 hours the next morning. Which was great and an exception, as usually on arrival at the mill you were told to get a move on. You were running late for your patrol! 90% of operations were taxied by helicopter, so punctuality was a given as Bessbrook's Helipad was the busiest helipad in Europe when we were there.

I was laid on my back, feet crossed, hands behind my head on the top bunk in our room, when Dave returned from his briefing, slapping my boots and telling Bash to leave is magazines alone.

Dave then got the maps out and spread them on his bunk. He said, "We had better take a good look at these men, its right on the border and we have not been there before."

He then smoothed the map over with his hands and turning to Bash said, "Last page of my notebook. There is a list of special sites and additional weapons plus extra first aid gear we are taking with us. Read the list back to me, then go and sign for them. Ask for them to be stored near our gats. I don't want to be fucking about at 3.30 a.m. tomorrow."

Bash opened the book and read '2 x 197 night sites, 1 x M79 grenade launcher, six x grenades, 2 x 9 mm browning pistols,' then toddled off to the armoury, probably dreaming about firing the M79.

"Steve, can you sort the extra first aid," asked Dave as he continued to sort the maps.

"Sure. No probs. I will nip and see Jock after this," I replied.

After the briefing and running about sorting everything, we all watched a bit of TV in the television room, grabbed a late lunch followed by some sleep, which none of us had got much of the last two weeks in Newry.

03.15 Hours Wednesday.

I HEARD OUR first alarm go off giving you five wonderful minutes before the next dreaded alarm played its tune. Dave and Bash were first out of the room to the showers followed by Chris and myself. It was amazing what a shower and a mug of tea could do.

Ten minutes in the shower and out, cleaned teeth, towel around my waist and back to the room to get dressed, Dave asked, "Who is going for weapons?"

"Bash and I will get 'em, Dave," I said pulling my Norwegian army shirt over my head, nice and warm those shirts with a polo neck and zipped collar. You didn't wear your flak jacket when on patrol in rural areas unless ordered.

"Chris will you nip to the kitchen and grab four hot sarnies, nothings ordered. I spoke to the cook yesterday and they have got thirty men coming in at 4.30am, so there will be someone in the mess."

"No problem, Dave," said Chris. "Any specific requests?"

Dave and I asked for bacon, and Bash came back with "Whatever you can fit in the bread!"

Chris left me and Bash sat on one of the bottom bunks of our ten foot x seven foot room. You heard right. That was the size, a full four foot square, less than a legal prison cell for two men. Not a problem really unless one of you has wind, and to be fare we weren't in them that much.

04.10 Hours

WE EXITED THE Mill by slamming shut the solid three inch steel vault door at top of the great stair case. This would automatically lock with a timing device. Starting our decent down the fire escape was always a concern as you could see the bullet holes in the walls were the IRA had taken shots at squaddies, when we noticed it was dry for once. (*Hurray*)

Dave leading was already half way down when he queried to us and probably himself, "No-one forgotten anything?"

No-one answered, so I guess we had everything, although Basher couldn't have answered if he had wanted to, as he was busy ramming in the last piece of his second sandwich into his mouth. We all lined up at the bottom of the stairs facing into the loading bay with our gats. Checking the chambers were empty, we loaded our magazines.

"Are we loading the Brownings Dave?" I enquired, as it was Dave and myself who were carrying the pistols.

Chris had the M79, Bash was our GPMG man, (general purpose machine gun) and that was heavy enough.

"We'll load them out of the building on patrol, Steve" Dave said as he tapped his jacket to feel the browning.

04.30 Hours Hells Road.

HELL'S ROAD WAS the nick name given to the short length of road commandeered by the army as it linked the mill and helipad. It was sealed off at either end and guards were placed there in Sangers. However, the IRA often just turned up and started firing down the road, causing all kinds of HELL to break loose, hence the name. We arrived through the barrier of were the helicopters lived. We did our final checks on our webbing to ensure it was all secure. Then not to disappoint, it started to piss down with Irish rain. Hastily, we made our Bergens waterproof, whilst at the same time keeping an eye on the Core Pilot to give us the go ahead to board.

I noticed the ground crew still filling up with fuel and the earth spikes were still connected so we had a few minutes. I glanced around and spotted two officers coming towards the helipad.

I shouted to Dave, "Do these two want us?"

He came over to me and said, "I'll see. If you board the bird, put my stuff on Steve. Cheers."

The reason they wouldn't come all the way to us was because the helicopter, or bird, as Dave liked to call them was warming up. This meant the blades were going around quite fast. With rain driven even more our way by the down draught of the blades, you didn't want to be on the helipad unless you had to.

Our brick was in stick formation, waiting to board,

which means you are down on one knee, head gear off and secured. One man behind the other facing the doors of the helicopter. At that moment, I was facing the Flight Marshall whilst trying to keep my head up in what was really driving torrential rain. Chris was looking past me in the direction of Dave talking to the two officers. They had been joined by a mysterious third man, who was wearing a Para smock and camouflage paint on his face. This was green, brown and black, which told us that this bloke was keen, to say the least. From where we were viewing the conservation it looked like this man had taken over and was trying to get something very important across to Dave.

It must have worked because Dave came running down to us at speed. He reached us, slightly out of breath, after all he had just done a one hundred foot sprint in full combats.

He said, "No-one board the bird except on my orders!"

He was then off again towards the helicopter which was now fuelled and ready to go.

I remember Chris saying to me, *'He looks like a mountain gorilla'*, which was because of the way you had to board the helicopter, your knees bent, back shoulders and head arched over, arms dragging still by your sides. We were still in stick formation, waiting anxiously as Dave tried to get the Marshall to cut the engine. Dave kept glancing at the three men who stood behind us, but the blades were still moving for take-off.

Just then the guy dressed in full camouflage ran passed us and just bending down slightly ran all the way to the helicopter, jumped into the side doors where the passengers board. You could see him pushing his head through to where the pilot sat and after a few seconds the bird slowed its wings down.

The Marshall climbed on board, and then I was distracted by Bash turning to Chris and me.

He started whining, "The fucking water is running down the crack of my arse."

The way he came out with it, his timing was perfect. Hell was about to break loose on the helipad. Yet, Bash totally oblivious to the emerging chaos, came out with one of his self-orientated one liners. Nearly all the ground crew was approaching the helicopter now.

One lieutenant ran up to us, "What the devilish hell is going on?" he screamed in an upper class tone.

"The fucking rain is running down my crack, Sir," Bash screamed at him.

I intervened and said, "You had better go speak to them, Sir," and pointed to the two officers who had been talking to Dave.

The Lieutenant gave Bash a very camp dissatisfied glance, then left as he went towards the more civilized officers. Glancing back at the helicopter, Mr Camouflage had the Flight Marshall by the throat. Dave was forcing himself between them both and shouted over for us. Leaving our gear, we ran to help.

"Get that daft cunt away from here," Dave said pointing with his hand and shaking his head towards the Flight Marshall.

Bash swung his arm around the Marshall's neck from the rear and put some pressure on the back of his knees.

"Who does he think he fucking is head butting me? I'll fucking have him," said the Marshall, trying to save face.

He was probably quite relieved we intervened. I don't think he would have really wanted to get into a fight, not looking at the state his nose was in, which wasn't pleasant to say the least. We got the Marshall, whose name we found out later was Gary, back to the helipads rest room. We sat him down and he started to shake and cry. (*Nothing girlish about that the after effects of adrenaline*) A couple of his work mates tried to console him and at the same time vigorously questioned us.

Just then, the Lieutenant entered the room and after taking one look at Gary's face and the amount of blood, he looked like he was starting to sway and turn pale. He needed to lean on a nearby filing cabinet to stop himself falling.

At that point amid all the commotion, I said to the Lieutenant,

"Sir, you'd better get this man to a Medic or a Medic to the man."

Looking very pale and shaken himself, he gave the order to the two men trying to calm Gary down.

"Private Kershaw, Private Green, take him to the Medic's room and then report back to me the outcome."

On cue and as thoughtful as ever Bash said to the Lieutenant, "Is the water running down your crack now, Sir?"

"What's your name, Soldier?" said the Lieutenant trying to sound confident and put Bash in his place.

He probably wouldn't have attempted to do this if he had known what Bash was like. I've seen him fork through a man's hand for trying to pinch a chip from his plate and literally bite some ones ear off because he called Bash a ginger nut. Bash had no conscience. *(We were his conscience)*

At this point Dave burst in, "Come on lads, we've got an urgent briefing in the QRF room." He then, realizing he had sort of interrupted the Lieutenant, saluted and apologized, the Lieutenant half returned the salute as we all strolled past him

05.25 Hours QRF Room.

WE SLUNG OUR jackets on the radiator and all sat down, praying the briefing would last long enough to dry them. We were talking amongst ourselves, speculating to what the fuck had gone wrong, enough to stop or ground a Wocker Wocker, (*helicopter*) when Dave came in followed by Mr Camouflage and the two mysterious officers. This actually made the room quite cramped. The quick reaction force room was only designed for four men to sleep in on bunk beds. There was a TV on a wall mounted stand in the far corner and a small table in the other corner with brew kit and a kettle on. A simple table which had been there from the 60's, very thin metal tubed legs and a speckled pale blue and white Formica top. The floor of the room was red lead paint, which now was like glass having been polished for decades. The walls were in total contrast been pale sky blue.

Dave gave us all a plastic cup and Mr. Camouflage followed him filling them up with coffee. He was apologising for delaying our patrol and causing a scene on the helipad.

Dave sat down on the bed next to us and one of the officers Captain Jones began to speak.

"Thank you men for sitting in on this briefing and remaining calm and cooperative earlier. The time is now 05.30 hours," he told us, glancing at his watch. Then continued, "You've been delayed an hour, and you will be delayed another hour whilst you are given a briefing. Following that, you will be asked to volunteer to make some adjustments to your next patrol. I must stress you are under no obligation to volunteer and I mean that. I will now hand you over to Trooper West," and pointed to Mr Camouflage.

"*SAS*", Chris and I said glancing at each other, smirking like kids who'd been given new bikes. To the average squaddie an SAS man was a God.

Bash then joined in saying, "That explains the head butt. Fucking brilliant. Your head hardly moved, and you must have broken his nose in two places"

Mr Camouflage picked up on what Bash said then spoke, "Bash is it? What happened earlier should not have happened. However, that Marshall will think twice next time before grabbing someone." Looking around at each of us he said, "Right, are there any more questions before I start? Also for the remainder of the brief please feel free to call me John."

At that, John spun around and started shaking the officers hands, thanked them for their help and cooperation. They left the room closing the door behind them. John turned back to face us and said,

"They are all right, but they don't like to get their hands dirty, if you know what I mean."

"I'll start by explaining the reason behind that incident on the helipad and also why you've been chosen as a brick." John made himself as comfortable as you possibly can, sat on one cheek on the corner of a small table. Chris bent down to pick up one of the jackets which had fallen on the floor and John's comment was,

"I wouldn't bother it's still pissing down outside. As you have already no doubt worked out, I'm a member of the SAS, and I've just got back off a four day patrol. Which I'm not proud to say didn't go very well. In fact it was a total fucking cock up!"

There was disgust in John's voice, he had another sip of coffee and then began "Well, I might as well start from the beginning, but I'll warn you all. This is Top Secret. Not that it matters. It will all be denied anyway, and as to what Captain Jones said about it being voluntary. Please do think about that because I've now got two men shot dead and one recovering in Hospital. Most important of all, there is one still out there who we know is injured, possibly dead, which unfortunately would be better for us. Well, the ones above me that is. The one still out there is only nineteen, and he has already been under cover for two years, due to a family connection. He was actually a twin, but separated at birth. Unfortunately his brother was shot, but we replaced him with his twin. Very deceitful we know." At this Bash and I grinned and looked at Chris.

"Mr X, as we will call him, was probably the most successful undercover agent we have had for about ten years. If he hadn't been discovered he would have done a certain terrorist movement a lot of damage," John said as he passed the flask to Dave, suggesting we topped up.

Just then a bang on the outside door! John went to open it but closed the internal door. He was back in seconds carrying an a3 flip chart on a stand. He erected the stand for the chart as we all sipped our coffee. He pulled up the outer cover of the A3 pad to reveal a map of virtually the same area our patrol was visiting.

"Have you got a route marked on your map of today's patrol?" John asked Dave.

"Yes," replied Dave.

Already getting our map out and following it to roughly the same area as the one on the chart. This route, as far as map reading goes, was quite easy to identify the patrol areas on because of two old ruins and some actual permanent points along the border. John passed over a sheet of transparent thin plastic to Dave. He asked if he could trace his route onto the sheet. Dave obliged and passed the sheet back. After clipping the sheet to the map, John opened his note book and copied six map reference numbers out of it onto the bottom of his chart. He then turned back to us.

"John, I have a question, if that's ok?" Chris said with his hand half up in the air.

"Fire away, if you forgive the expression." John replied.

"Well, just quickly working out the numbers you have put on the chart they are virtually parallel with our route. Is this a coincidence or what?"

John came straight back and complimented Chris's speed of working out the coordinates.

"In fact, if you don't mind just pop up here and put a little circle where you worked out each of the points, Chris." The room went quiet and bash shouted teacher's pet.

Handing his cup of coffee to me, he went to the front and took the marker pen John handed to him. He started to draw. He commented to John that he had only worked out the numbers to six digits and not eight.

"I'm still impressed," said John.

"So am I," said Dave.

After Chris sat back down, John turned back to face the board and clipped another transparent sheet over the map. John's new sheet was marked with six black dots, and each one was smack in the middle of Chris's circles.

John commented, "Well in fifteen years of military

service, six of them in the SAS. I've never seen anything as good as that where map reading is concerned. Back to your question, half-way through your patrol your brick would have received a radio message asking you to check the area. Conveniently, one of the Protestant Terrorist Groups would have claimed an ambush on the IRA. Your brick would have confirmed this fact and a clear up operation would have started. This is the reason, in case you were wondering, why your brick as had such a large gap before your first patrol. We needed to get our timings aligned and make sure you were rested."

It was now totally day light outside and the rain had eased, but looked far from stopping.

John continued, "As to these references that I have marked, they are all possible points where our Mr X may hold up. If he is still alive!"

Just then another bang on the door. John went to answer it, this time leaving the internal door open. We could see that Private Kershaw was standing there handing John a piece of paper.

"Thanks," John said and taking a step back into the building as not to get the note wet.

He read it. Which didn't take long then turning straight to us he said, "You have six minutes. The Lynx that has just landed is yours. Make a note of these coordinates, and three hours into your patrol when you make your first radio check. If you are going to do the search, confirm to Captain Jones the weather is ok. If you decide against the search, just tell him the weather has worsened. The two references that are in red are just across the border, so make sure your lost if you check the red two. Thanks lads and good luck," John said packing up his gear. We all exited the QRF room shaking Johns hand as we passed.

06.20 Hours 100ft above Bessbroke.

WE GAINED HEIGHT in the Lynx, and Dave started to discuss the Landing Zone with the Core Pilot. He familiarised himself with the ground as the air force maps had much greater detail regarding the level of the Terrain and anyone who's visited Ireland they will know it's a hill on top of a hill. It is a beautiful place and if the conflict/war were not going on the tourist trade would be I am sure booming and the majority of people there are lovely. Fifteen minutes into the flight, our bird carried out a steep descent into a green field. Below us, the sheep seemed to scatter like bits of fluff.

Coming into land, we opened the doors at thirty feet, the wind and weather blowing in. Bash and I removed our headsets as we would be first out to give the helicopter cover. That was also the reason for the very steep descent. We moved that close to the border the IRA had a perfect opportunity to shoot down a British helicopter using 50 mm Browning's. They had so far hit a couple but not brought one down.

When we made touchdown, Bash jumped out left. I dived right. Dave and Chris got all the gear out and lay across it, so the down draft from the blades did not blow any away.

In less than a minute, the helicopter only resembled a faint dot in the sky. The Bird safely out of range of any attacks. Dave and Chris slung their rifles around their backs, picked up two Bergens each and ran to the edge of the field into the bush line. As they settled themselves, they covered us as we ran to join them. The weather had actually started to brighten up. The rain had stopped and the sun was trying it's best to get through. Bash was now tucked nicely into the edge and keeping look out in the direction from which we had come. I was covering left and rear. Chris was taking care of the right and rear.

Dave had the map out and was orientating it to the ground, when he suddenly looked up and said, "I'm going for the extra duties, but I also respect anyone that doesn't want to do it. We won't either unless the full brick is unanimous."

Chris looked at me and I nodded, "We're all in Dave," Chris said.

"Right 5 m spread. Steve, can you keep the rear?" asked Dave.

"Sure. No probs," I answered as I helped Chris put his Bergen on.

"We will patrol for two and a half hours and should be in sight of the river. We will make our radio check there and grab a bite to eat."

Chris interrupting Dave at this point saying, "I'm sure John will be glad to hear the weather is okay."

We all laughed and moved off in good spirits. There was no need to ask Bash we knew he would follow us 3 through the front door of Lucifer's house that was Bash.

09.25 Hours

WE'D BEEN WALKING for well over two hours and carrying full gear, which weighed over one hundred and fifty pounds. Dave made the sign that we would be stopping and pointed to a wooded area, then signed to stop and take cover. We all moved into the side of a three foot stone wall. The next command was Dave touching the top of his beret and making the number two with his fingers. This meant he wanted Chris to come to him. It was routine, and he would want Chris to dump his gear and carry out a rekey of the wooded area.

Bash watching what was happening, adjusted the site of the GPMG to bring the wood into range, which would enable covering fire to be put down if Chris came under attack. Within twenty-five minutes, we had all moved into the wood, secured a perimeter and got some food on the boil.

Dave was on the radio reporting that Delta One was on schedule and all was okay. After relaying the message the weather was ok for Captain Jones, he signed off D1 out. After filling our stomachs with boiled rice and chicken in brown sauce with a black mug of coffee, Dave gathered Chris and me around for a small briefing regarding the alterations to the patrol. Bash was on stag (*guard duty*) and would have to be briefed later.

04.15 Present Day
North Ferriby, Hull.

ARTHUR AND I pulled into the car park at North Ferriby, Arthur enquired if I was on the telephone and was quite astonished when I told him, "No."

"What not even a mobile phone?" Arthur quizzed.

"Not even one of those," I replied as we pulled up next to my car.

"Just open that first aid box that is under your seat and grab the little black leather case thing," Arthur said as he switched off the engine and twisted in his seat towards me.

With the box on my knee, I popped the lid open expecting to view a first aid kit, but to my surprise, I was staring down at a fair wad of cash in different currencies; including English pounds, Spanish pesetas, Dutch guilders and German Marks. Underneath were about six brown envelopes containing something bulky. Next to the cash were five or six small objects in different shaped containers. Arthur said, "Take the one with the pressed stud fastening."

Realising I was struck dumb. Arthur butted in with, "It's my life and movement First aid. I am sure there is a couple of Elastoplast's in there somewhere. Pass it over here. It's a bleeper. I'll check it, switch it on and you can borrow it until you get sorted with a phone."

Arthur took the bleeper out of its case I said, "Thanks Arthur. Just one more question… What about payment?"

"Left the best to last, eh Steve? Normally, you claim your petrol and expenses when you are in the office, but the wages are usually sent through the post to your home address by way of a cheque or you can have them bank transfer. It usually takes about three to four weeks after the job. I take it Chris and Bash didn't pass that bit of information on." Arthur finished

"No. I think they were just glad to get me some work. It doesn't matter. It will be nice when it comes."

Seeing my look of disappointment, Arthur said, "Pass me the English cash from the box."

"No… No. I'm not hinting. It's just if I get any more jobs through Dave, I will need my car, and it's not taxed or insured."

"One thing at a time Steve. You are insured. If you get stopped or anything like that call the number scratched on the bleeper, and in the meantime, I will drop a policy off for you. This is for you to show and you just say you work for Delta 1 Security. Our insurance will cover you. As far as your road tax is concerned, leave it with me for day or two, and just park carefully."

Stretching out his hand to me Arthur insisted I take the cash as he held out, "There's £240 Steve. I've deducted £20 for your tax. I will put the double trip down in my name for this one and maybe the next couple I will be able to get you some cash, but you will have to sort something out with Dave regarding future payments," Arthur told me.

Thanking Arthur, I started to get out of the car

when he stopped me saying, "One last thing Steve. The bleeper vibrates as well, and if it does go off, ring the number on the side."

Once again, I thanked Arthur and pushed the door closed. (*Smiling as I just kept thinking Dave as named his company after our brick from Northern Ireland.*)

Back in my own car reality struck home. Probably because it took five minutes to start my engine, and I was frozen. Then, sitting there for another five minutes letting the car warm up, I noticed the time was 05.20 hours. Instead of driving home, I made my way three or four miles up the motorway to the South Cave turning, which led to the site I was working at. (*South Cave Castle*) I was too high to sleep anyway, fuck me for once in what felt like a decade I was living.

13.17 Hours (building site)

It was just before lunch, I had a twenty-one foot steel scaffolding tube in my hands, when I felt a slight vibration in my chest pocket. Quickly clipping the tube in place, I said to the labourer who was helping me that I was off to the fish shop for lunch and did he want anything?

"My treat," I said.

"Patty and chips, if your flush Steve," he answered.

I was gone in thirty seconds and walking to the nearest telephone. I was once again starting to feel the adrenalin kick in. After dialling the number on the bleeper as instructed, a voice came on to the other end of the line saying, "Calls to this number are being diverted. Please hold the line."

This message started to repeat when it rang again. I prepared myself for the two James Bond ladies, who I spoke to on my first contact when the phone was answered, "Dave Sissons."

"Dave, its Steve. Steve Lewis," I told him eagerly on hearing my old friend's voice.

"Steve… My man. At last we speak. How are you?" Dave asked

"Great now I'm earning a bit extra. Thanks to you, and you know who." Dave knew I was referring to Chris and Bash.

"Yes, they said you were having a bit of bad luck. Hang on a minute. How did you get this number?" Dave asked surprised.

Before I had chance to answer, I heard Arthur in the background asking if it was me on the phone and explaining his mobile was on divert.

Apologising Dave said, "Things are apparently moving faster than I knew where you are concerned. In fact, Arthur and I are in a meeting at the moment, and you were the next on the agenda. Are you in a call box Steve?"

"Yes and I haven't a lot of change left." I told him

"Give me the number and I will ring you back," said Dave.

I read the number to him when the blips started and the phone went dead. It was about five minutes before the phone rang again.

Instantly picking up the receiver I heard Dave asking for me.

"It's Steve speaking, Dave."

"Are you busy tonight?" Dave came back with.

"Another airport run?" I suggested.

"Fuck me, no! I don't deal with the day to day stuff Steve. No… Arthur has got a couple of operations coming up, and he would like to offer you a position in them. He has been asking me if I would vouch for you. Tell you what Steve, if you are free tonight, make your way to the taxi office, but don't park outside the front. Drive to the rear of the office. It looks like a disused underground car park. Just press your horn three times and someone will let you in. We will need you to arrive at around 18.30 hours. There will be a few tests you need to go through. Nothing to worry about. At about 21.30 hours come with Arthur to my place and stop the night. I will have a spare room made up. I've got another guest coming for drinks. Talk about a coincidence. I think you will remember him. Anyway see you tonight Steve."

Dave put the phone down and I walked to the fish shop puzzled, thinking tests, spare room, and guest?

18.15 Hours

REAR OF DAVE'S office, Bradford, I remembered my horn didn't work. So I got out of my car and banged with the bottom of my fist three times on the large steel roller, shutter door. Not hanging around, I got back into my car, not just because the rain had just started again, but because the area I was in resembled a cross between the Bronx and a war time England. Then, with my window down, I heard the shutter doors start to shake and make a loud clicking noise.

There was the humming of a very powerful motor as the door opened to about four feet, when the motor stopped and a uniformed guard bending down came from underneath. The guard placed a hat on his head and proceeded to my car.

"Could you dip your lights? Please, sir?"

I concurred and switched my lights to parked setting.

"Thank you, Sir," he replied. He was about two feet in front of my vehicle and bending slightly, checking my registration against his clip board in his left hand. He then came round to my side, "Mr Lewis, I believe sir?"

"Yes, Stephen Lewis," I answered. Then said "Call me Steve, not sir please."

Taking what looked like a small remote control from his clip board, he aimed it at the door, and the shutter door started to open again. The guard, leaning closer to me, gave me instructions to follow the green light until I could see two green lights together. I was then to park there on that level and someone would come to greet me. He wished me a good night and walked towards the door. He waved as I drove by.

I must have driven thirty feet when I was at a junction of three entrances. The right one had a yellow and red light above, the centre had a blue and white light, and the left which was obviously my turning had a green and amber light above. I followed the light code going up spirally, for I believe three levels when the amber light disappeared. Following the guard's instructions, I continued until I saw two green lights.

The light grey, bare smooth concrete walls were on this level all now painted in red/ blue with a black stripe along the top/middle and bottom, as well as coloured lights at each turning. This level had like electric cats eyes set in the floor, which in some magical way seemed to pull you in that direction. The only other lights around were small fan shaped up lighters. Next to the fire extinguishers and welcome signs, which were in four different languages? There was also a variety of hanging baskets containing what I presume, must have been artificial flowers due to the fact there was no sunlight. The guarding lights which were now set into the wall of each parking bay were both green. There must have been about fifteen bays, but to give you some idea of the size of this level. If this had been your average car park there would have been sixty plus parking bays.

In the far corner, I could see two Range Rovers with blacked out windows and private registration plates 'DELTA 1 and DELTA 4'. Opposite these, was a silver limousine again with blacked out windows and a couple of bays to the left of the limousine were two BMW motorcycles (not little ones). Just as I switched off my engine, because of the seriously expensive cars, I asked myself, '*Did the guard say green?*'

As I sat there, the far corner near the Range Rover's lit up and simultaneously two sliding doors opened along with the rear door of one of the Range Rover's. Squeezing out of the Range Rover then was two of the biggest Iraq men I'd ever seen. Both wearing dark suits and white granddad shirts with no ties short smart haircuts, menacing square heads. They went to meet a smaller Iraq gentleman coming out of the elevator with Arthur and I was ninety percent sure also Dave.

The two large foreign men stood in front of the smaller Iraqi gentleman and started pointing to Arthur. Then he turned and pointed to me in my car. He was well aware of the fact that I'd arrived after them and hadn't yet got out of my vehicle. At that point Arthur came across to me, so I opened the door to greet him.

Still in my tatty overalls I said, "What the fucking hell is this place?" (*Quietly of course*)

Tapping me on the shoulder, Arthur informed me, "This is your mates business. Part of it anyway."

We then started towards the Iraqi's and Dave.

"Just wing it Steve. For ten minutes, play it by ear. Then you will get the guarded tour," whispered Arthur.

We got within two feet of the party at the elevator, and Dave said to me, "Good operation, Steve."

"No problems," I replied.

Dave then said to Hamid, the small Iraqi, "Undercover jobs cost a fortune to make them look authentic. Take that car for instance. Looks like a clapped out Ford Mondeo, when in fact it's just had five grand spent on it. (*Mechanical and surveillance*) Which as you can see, did not include a paint job." Dave finished speaking with a courteous chuckle.

Dave cupping Hamid's hand in an affectionate, but business like way said, "Farewell," and assured him he would take over the operation they'd discussed as soon as the plane landed. Hamid responded with his thanks and farewells.

The Range Rover pulled away and we entered the lift.

"You've put a bit of weight on since I last saw you," said Dave.

"Yes, I've been weight training seriously for about six years now, I replied taking what Dave said as a compliment.

"No wonder Arthur wants you on his surveillance section. How's your fitness Steve?"

"Not bad but it has been better." I replied as I was thinking, '*Fuck me! You have changed Dave.*'

"Just that you will be tested on it tonight. Steve. Arthur is going to give you a little tour of the place, and he will take charge of the tests. I apologise, but I really must shoot off as I've got some people coming tonight. In fact, did I mention you might know one of them?" Dave did sound in a rush.

"Steve, thanks for coming. Catch you tonight, and we will have a chat, drink and something to eat."

Turning to Arthur, "See you about 21.30 hours at my place," Dave instructed as he was stepping out of the lift.

"Yes, Dave," answered Arthur, with a sarcastic

salute. At that, Dave was gone making his way to the remaining Range Rover. The elevator doors slid shut and to my amazement the reverse of the doors were mirrored. This meant the full interior of the lift was all mirrored, and no door joining was visible.

"Impressive, Steve isn't it?" Arthur said.

"You're telling me," I replied.

"It's all to impress our clients. Most of them are something to do with eastern oil producing countries, apart from what we call the evolved cases!"

"Evolved?" I questioned.

"All in good time... All in good time," replied Arthur cutting me off dead.

The lift stopped. Arthur about turned and a different two mirrors opened.

We walked out into, I guess, a working general office of about six desks, three of which were manned. There was two middle aged females and one man aged about sixty.

One of the ladies looked up saying, "You're working late, Arthur, and who's your mate? Big lad isn't he?"

"Behave yourself Alice. He's too young for you," Arthur replied in a friendly manner.

I just stayed stum (quiet). We left the office pushing aside to pine swinging doors.

Arthur commented, "That was Alice, Steve. Apart from me and Dave, of course, she has been with the firm the longest. She's usually the second voice you hear on the telephone giving you orders."

Arthur pushed open another set of doors, then talked again, "You would never have guessed listening to her on the phone and then meeting her in person would you, Steve?"

"No way. I had her down as a sophisticated official militarised secretary, not a down to earth Geordie with a fading accent," I replied.

"I couldn't have described her better myself," laughed Arthur.

"One more thing, if you are ever in trouble out on a job and you can't get in touch with Dave or myself, she is totally trust worthy and could probably solve a lot of situations." Arthur said this with genuine respect for Alice.

Stopping half way down the corridor, Arthur turned left and pushed open a door. We entered into a small room facing four large windows, where you could see a man and a woman playing squash quite competitively. Arthur leaned quite close to the window and speaking into a small microphone, pressed the button and said, "Sarah, Steve's here when you are ready."

At that, the woman playing squash put her hand up towards the glass to suggest five more minutes. Coming back to me Arthur sat down on a spectator's type bench and I joined him.

"That's the Queen Bee, Steve, or at least that's what the lads call her, but not to her face I may add. Her name is Sarah Kennedy. She is the company's fitness instructor. Not quite a full woman. Some of the lads have suggested, but that's probably because she has turned them down, and no doubt their pride has been hurt. You may even meet her again after the tests tonight at Dave's. She often visits his place to use his firing range and don't let that soft female shell fool you. She is also a qualified CPO and a very good one. She has been with us for two years after leaving the Police Force under a bit of a cloud. She had put her ex-sergeant in hospital for a week after he got off with sexual harassment charges."

Just then the door at the end of the viewing room opened and into the room entered Sarah. She had put on a loose fitting cotton top which quickly absorbed the sweat from the parts of her body, which the tight top she had played squash in didn't touch.

Wiping her forehead with a small white towel she came over to us.

"Hi, Arthur," she said slightly out of breath in a posh Scottish accent.

The man Sarah had been playing squash with followed her through the door, wearing a towel around his neck and breathing much more deeply than Sarah. He walked passed us and dripping in sweat.

"Fitness program working then Darren?" Arthur said.

Before Darren had chance to answer Arthur, "Same time tomorrow, Darren, and don't be late," Sarah remarked this time in a much broader authoritative Scottish accent.

"Still treating them rough I see, Sarah," Arthur said

smiling.

"You know what they are like," Sarah answered back in her sweet voice. "Right down to business. Follow me, Steve. Do you know what a bleep test is?" she asked as I followed her.

I replied, "Is it where you run between two points, increasing your pace on each length until you miss the buzzer?"

"Perfect, except on ours, you have got set number of seconds to press a light at each end and you are allowed three misses, then the test is over. *Clear*?" She spoke very assertively.

"*Clear*," I replied.

Sarah demonstrated how to press the lights which were at each end of the squash court, built in sets of four. So I guess you could have four people doing the test at any one time.

"I will expect twenty-five Steve, but don't overdo it. It's an assessment remember, not a test."

She closed the door on her way out and went to re-join Arthur. They left me standing there, anxiously waiting for the light to turn red. Twenty-nine and I was finding it difficult. Thirty-two and I just wanted two more. I'd already missed two lights, so with one more chance, I kept running. Thirty-six and the pace was virtually sprinting, nearly collapsing to my knees. I slapped my hands against the wall, kissing the cold plaster with my cheek and gasping for breath.

Arthur and Sarah entered.

"A gutsy performance Steve, but plenty of room for

improvement on the actual aerobic side of things."

I gave her a stern but tired look.

"Follow me for the multi-gym test, power and all that," was said as she led me to the next test.

I followed Sarah. Arthur patted me on the back and handed me a towel. Sarah was filling in a chart of some sort, as I felt my breath resuming back to normal. The multi-gym room was about twenty feet by fifteen feet and decorated in a yellow and orange colour scheme, with a full wall mirrored. The machines in the room were for full body work outs, a couple of leg presses, a peck deck for your chest, and tucked under the mirrors was a rack of dumbbells.

"This assessment is all to do with power in your legs, back, chest, and upper body, Steve," said Sarah.

"At least I will get full points on this one. Don't be over confident," she tried to remind me.

"Not possible. Anything to do with weights turns me on," I said.

Arthur was chuckling away to himself.

"Do you see the bench press machine? Please sit on it, Steve," Sarah asked in a School Principal manner.

"What I need on this one is for you to choose a weight and carry out ten repetitions with the last two being a struggle. Please carry on when you are ready." Sarah finished talking and glanced down at her chart.

I turned my attention to the weights and took the pin out of the thirty kilogram slot and pushed it in at the bottom which was seventy-five kilograms.

"Remember ten reps, Steve," she said as if she

needed to remind me. Standing up, I walked over to the dumbbell rack and picked up two thirty kilogram dumbbells. I then returned to the press machine, lying back down on the bench press. I gripped both the dumbbells and the press. This was made easier because on a multi-gym the pressing bar being shaped like a Y.

I pressed a comfortable ten and sat up saying, "If you want my maximum for ten. I would add another twenty kilograms to that say about one hundred and fifty-five kilograms."

I took the dumbbells back, and she must have seen me smiling in the mirrors.

"Legs, Steve!" She said not cross, secretly surprised.

"What have you got on the large press there?" I asked pointing to the larger of the two presses.

"Two hundred kilograms, and I suppose that's not enough," Sarah said sweetly.

"Well, eighteen months ago I pulled a bus for charity. A double decker with 30 kids on it. My training for that involved step ups with three hundred and fifty kilograms and half squats with four hundred kilograms. This is a fitness room not a weight room to me."

"What about arms?" asked Sarah.

"Last November I broke the Yorkshire curling record and only just failed the British record." She looked at Arthur and looking down at her chart, ticked the four boxes.

"Follow me, and well done, Steve. A very good show of strength," Sarah remarked in her posh Scottish accent.

"Fighting Steve. Have you had any formal training for me to work with?" Sarah asked with a bit of cheek.

"I've done some boxing and some Aikido, plus sparing with Dave. Which believe me is formal." I laughed and then said, "He is a hard lad."

"Well, don't think size is everything," she said as she pushed open another pine door leading us into an open gymnasium with fight mats already laid out on the floor forming a twenty foot square arena. Dropping our kit and other belongings at the side of the mats, it was clear that these mats were regularly fought on. They were well worn, and I couldn't count the blood stains!!

After fifteen minutes of taking a beating, I thought her nick name of 'Queen Bee' came from her punches stinging! Being fair to Sarah, she was good. Not just as an instructor. I reckon she could hold her own in a real scrap.

Arthur said, "Right thanks, Sarah. We are off to the weapons simulator. I will look forward to receiving your report." Sarah stood there drying herself off asked Arthur.

"What position is he coming in for?"

"Well, he'll be doing spare man on a couple of my jobs for now. I hope to send him on a full CPO course in about six months and start some in-house to get him up to speed for the big evolved job that the Brigadier as lined up."

"Is that wise? I thought we only tuck on CPO recruits from military or similar backgrounds?" Sarah asked cautiously.

Then she asked again, "Evolved operations? Dave won't have that Arthur."

"He is ex-army and his references don't come much higher. You'll see." Arthur said as he glanced my way. Then he asked Sarah "Are you using Dave's range tonight?"

"I don't think so. I would like to I have a run and shoot contest coming up, but I think he's got some guests coming Arthur,"

"Thanks for your time, Steve," Sarah said bending down and putting her stuff in her sports bag.

"No problem. Thanks for the demonstration of girl power, and I will be bruised for a week." I smiled and said goodbye.

Walking down the corridors with Arthur he said, "You will like this next bit Steve. It's a weapon range simulator, one of the most advanced in the world." We got it as a gift from one of the Saudi's royal family, after Dave prevented a kidnapping of their son.

We stopped outside two doors, and Arthur started to punch in some numbers on a security entry panel at the side of the door. Walking into the room was like entering a television producer's room. There were four small monitors a couple of key pads and what looked to be hundreds of switches and lights built into a state of the art desk. Arthur sat on one of the chairs in front of the monitors and pressed a few switches and lights illuminated all over. Arthur loaded four CD's/ DISCS into magically appearing slots in the desk.

My eyes swept around the room which was in semi darkness. Arthur and I were in the left corner of a much larger room than I first thought. Just then as a few more lights were switched on, the far wall which was the size of a multi complex cinema screen, lit up.

"Ah, that's it," said Arthur chuffed with himself.

Swivelling around on his chair Arthur spoke, "Open those drawers behind you, Steve. There are three different pistols, browning, colt, and magnum. Do you have a preference?"

"No, not really, but I've only ever fired the browning," I answered, as I felt the weight of each weapon.

"That's right. Browning are army issue, and Dave always uses the browning."

I picked up the browning and checked the breach was empty.

"Grab a pair of ear defenders as well," said Arthur as he walked towards me with a couple of magazines in his hands.

"What does it fire, Arthur?" I enquired.

"Live rounds, Steve. Just that the velocity is drastically reduced and the head of the round is slightly flattened, similar to the dumb dumb bullet."

"Thanks," I said as I took the magazines.

"Don't load until you hear me say load and tell you the range is live," said Arthur as he opened the glass door part of the glass walls protecting the control room from the range. The thickness of the glass was at least twenty-five millimetres, which would have stopped most conventional rounds, never mind a reduced velocity one, but I guess it's better to be safe than sorry. I stood on a blue spot which had start written on it.

I heard Arthur's voice come over a speaker saying,

"Your first magazine will be expended on the following moving targets for you to become familiar with the weapon. Whilst the range is live, I should mention all standard safety precautions will be observed by you, is that clear?"

I raised my left hand to show I understood, Then I heard, "In your own time carry on live range."

I loaded the browning and took aim, and fired a round into each of the different shaped targets that were floating around the screen.

"11 hits, one miss, reload," Arthur's voice instructed.

'Not bad', I thought as I hadn't fired a shot in over ten years. I had just reloaded when on screen came the scene of a really packed shopping Centre/ Mall. The scene had incorporated the floor, ceiling and side walls of the range room. It was out of this world. I thought I had been beamed of the Star Ship Enterprise into the middle of Harrods, when without warning my body hit the back wall as the floor was moving. (Surreal)

"You have to walk. I told you it was good. Now, concentrate Steve. I need a good score on this one," was the commentary from the viewing room.

Arthur's voice went quiet and the sound of shoppers, tills, elevators and background music replaced the vacuum of silence. (*Out of this world*) Then, I started to receive instructions through my ear defenders.

Apparently, I was the main bodyguard and directly behind me was the Principal I was in charge of. He was a well-known minister, who had just wrote a controversial novel regarding Israel, which had angered a number of Israelis, a well-known terrorist group had promised to silence him for good and a bounty of one million pounds sterling! Had been put on his head. I had been walking through the shopping mall for around 5 minutes and by now I really believed I was there, especially with instructions being received from other CPO's, who I could actually see dotted around the centre.

Just then, out of the blue, a female officer ran from my right to another officer. They were about one hundred yards in front, and they were apprehending someone with difficulty.

I slowed my pace and instinctively opened my arms to protect my Principle, "Number 1. Number 1," I heard in my ear.

"The man we have just detained is of Israeli origin, armed and carrying a two way radio … I repeat armed,"

"Keep closer to me, Sir." I found myself actually saying out loud.

The female CPO came back into my ear saying, "I'm back and covering your right flank," with crackling from the receiver.

I was now breathing heavily and pumped up with adrenalin, but very much in control of my now heightened senses. (*Fucking alive I felt*)

Four more paces, and I noticed to my right a female cleaner in blue overalls. She was wearing high healed cowboy type boots. Keeping an eye on her she suddenly turned and was holding a pistol with a silencer on. I levelled my browning and put two rounds into her shoulder and chest.

The figure vaporized instantly, and the lights came on followed by Arthur's voice over the mike saying,

"Calm down, Steve. Face front and carry out unloading procedure."

It might sound daft him requesting me to calm down, but believe me, that was so fucking realistic. Pointing the weapon at the front wall I released the magazine, titled the fire arm and ejected the round which was in the chamber. Then aiming at the wall pulled the trigger to release the firing mechanism, resulting in a made safe weapon. More lights came on, and I started to debrief my own head. I mean I began to rationalize what I was doing and were I was.

Coming out of the glass door, Arthur kept saying, "Excellent, excellent. Come on lets watch the replay. Put your browning away and give me the magazines and spare rounds whilst the recording rewinds."

Opening the drawer, I replaced the weapon and ear defenders.

"Nice touch with the ear defenders," I commented as I turned to pass the magazines to him.

We both sat down in front of the monitors and as he pushed and pressed a couple of switches. One of the middle monitors came on, and we were able to view what had happened, showing a shot from behind me. I was astonished by the whole evening, but the simulator was the icing on the cake. Then, Arthur freeze framed the video and zoomed in on the other CPO's arresting the Israeli. You could see the struggle as well as the female CPO speaking into her mouth piece. That's when I had received the message about the perpetrator being armed. Pressing another switch on the monitor, the film restarted, coming to the vital part.

Arthur asked me, "How did you know to turn and keep an eye on the cleaner?"

"The boots, not the sort of footwear I would have associated with a store cleaner. All day in them… don't think so," I answered, not taking my eyes off the scene. "Fuck me. It looks real," I told him.

"That's why the shot person is removed instantly," Arthur said.

"What about the one I missed?" I questioned him.

"You didn't miss him. He was put in to show you the importance of a CPO team. It's not just one big man on his own anymore. Not when you are out in an environment like that Steve. You will need a team of at least three, possibly four. Right that's it for tonight. I make the time 20.30 hours, and its half an hour's drive to Dave's," Arthur said as he shut down the desk and room. Darkness returned as he turned out all the lights, and we exited.

Outside the room. Arthur tapped numbers again into the keypad. Whilst doing this he spoke, "We will go in my car and I will drop you back here in the

morning Steve… Steve!" Arthur had to raise his voice.
I was silent for a moment… mesmerised by everything
that had just taken place.

"Yes, Arthur," I finally said.

We exited the building with Arthur tapping numbers into several key pads and turning off the remaining
lights. Apparently, we were the last ones to leave.

21.20 Hours

WE'D BEEN DRIVING for approximately twenty to
twenty-five minutes when Arthur indicated and slowed
right down. He turned into what I call a tractor road,
(country lane) then drove five more minutes. We
turned again off this minor country lane and drove
onto a gravelled drive through a small wooded area.
The drive seemed to widen as we came out of the
trees. And there it was. Lit up like a work of art in a
gallery.

"That's not Dave's house is it?" I asked.

"Yes, that's it, Steve. Dave's mini mansion as he
calls it," replied Arthur.

It was an especially dark night, with no real moon,
and no street lights for miles. All this just multiplied the
effect. It was truly magnificent. There were eight
beams of light illuminating the front of the building. As
we drove even closer, you could make out the statue in
the centre of a circular stone fountain. It was a female
goddess figure. She was holding a large shell and
gracefully leaning forward with one of her legs was
bent backwards. The shell was tipped at a specific angle

allowing the water to cascade.

To add to the aquatic splendour, there were around thirty jets of water shooting into the centre of the fountain, terminating at the feet of the goddess. All the water was complemented by a gorgeous yellow light which seemed to grace the whole fountain and interacted perfectly with the water, yet you could not see where the source of the light crept into the fountain.

Dave's Range Rover was parked at an obscure angle, approximately fifteen feet to the right of the fountain. We parked next to this and got out of the Audi. I wandered over to take a closer look at the goddess, whilst Arthur grabbed our gear out of the boot. Luckily, I had left my suit in my car from the night before. (*Remember*) I had stopped on the way to purchase bits and bobs (*toothbrush / smalls and a clean pair of socks*).

Walking up the stone steps to the matching stone veranda, I was struggling to take it all in. The place was proper posh. Arthur realized I was distracted and led me in the direction he was going.

Then, the large main door opened and we were greeted by an elderly Chinese lady, "Welcome. Welcome, Arthur," said Marley. Then, he bent forward tried to kiss her cheek. Marley was having none of it and shoved him away. Arthur was laughing and Marley was flustered.

At this point, an old Chinese gentleman came to the door.

"Ah… it's you, Mr Arthur. I should have known with all the fuss Marley was making." The Chinese gentle man genuinely seemed pleased to see him.

"How are you Chang?" asked Arthur as they shook hands, bowing slightly.

"This is, Steve" said Arthur turning towards me. "Dave's expecting us for the night."

"Yes, Mr Arthur and three more people will be arriving."

"Three more?" enquired Arthur.

"Yes, there will be a late arrival of guests," replied Chang.

"I have put you in your usual room Mr. Arthur, and Mr. Steve is next door." "Thank you, Chang," replied Arthur, nudging me to follow as we entered the mansion through the large arched door way.

We walked through the doors and into the hall, and I noticed the care taken to restore the original authentic features. There were large portrait paintings of both male and females from a variety of centuries. There was a very large prominent oak staircase with a York stone floor. A suit of armour with several weapons, from I guess the same era as the suit, stood proudly on guard in the corner of the room. There were a couple of large story telling tapestry wall hangings, and selection of stuffed animal heads. At this point Dave came through a door across the hall.

"Is it that time already?" asked Dave surprised to see us.

"Thanks for coming Steve at such short notice."

"No problem. I wouldn't have missed this for the world. What a stunning place you have here, Dave," I informed him.

"Oh, and Steve. I heard you were showing off in the weight gym earlier tonight," commented Dave with a smirk.

"I take it Sarah's here then?" jumped in Arthur.

"Yes... she told me you had practically begged her to come," said Dave.

"Well it saved you coming up with an excuse to get her here." Arthur said laughing. "I don't know why you don't tell her how you feel. It's bloody obvious she feels the same way mate." Marley nodded her head in agreement.

"Sarah was wondering who had put the references up for you, Steve. You should've seen her face when I said you were the one who saved our Brick in Ireland," Dave said, attempting to divert the conversation.

"I don't know what you're talking about, Dave. I remember you taking two out with your Browning."

Arthur interrupted saying, "Before you two start reminiscing, tell me who are the other guests that are coming?" Arthur sounded like a child nagging.

"John, Tanya and the Brigadier," informed Dave.

Just as Dave finished talking, a loud low toned bell sounded. Marley instinctively went to answer the main door again. (Funny sight as the door was twice the size of her.) We turned to the door and watched as a male and female entered carrying their small overnight bags.

Dave moved towards them saying, "John, Tanya...

nice of you to come tonight. I know you are busy people, and we didn't give you a lot of notice. I'm sure you will understand why after the briefing... that is if the Brigadier as not informed you already." Whilst Dave was speaking, Tanya gave Marley a hug.

Dave then said,

"John, you remember Steve, don't you?"

"Of course, nice to see you, Steve. You have filled out nicely since we last met," said John as he leaned forward to shake my hand.

I moved a couple of steps towards him, and we shook hands. The moment I shook John's hand it was if I travelled back in time. My mind instantly thought back ten years to the day we had the briefing in the QRF room (Besbrook mill).

"It's been a long a long time John. You look really well. Is life treating you good?" I asked.

"Yes, Steve. It has been a long time... too long. And, life is good. I can't complain,"

John answered as he let go of my hand.

Arthur interrupted, "And the lovely girl standing next to him is Tanya. She's the brigadier's body guard. I'm only kidding. She's his PA, but say anything against the brigadier and she will kill you."

I was now getting used to Arthur's comments (however he was not far wrong with that one). Still standing near to John, I again reached out my hand this time to shake Tanya's.

"Nice to make your acquaintances, Steve," she said with a perfect smile.

I was about to say that it was nice to meet her as well... but no. My stupid male brain decided to come out with a clever comment, which did not sound as it did in my head.

I looked straight at Tanya and said, "Now I can see what inspired the fountain outside." It went fucking silent in the hall. I could see Arthur was dying to say something.

Tanya, bless her, at this point touched the back of my hand saying, "Thanks Steve," with a giggle. Then all of them started laughing.

Tanya spoke with a lovely soft strange, posh cockney accent. A petite woman standing about five feet four inches tall looking a bit oriental, I think. She had a feminine, but athletic figure. Her hair was light brown and fell to her shoulders. I found her very attractive.

After letting go of my hand, she went straight to Chang, and gave him a real hug not a welcome artificial one. These two knew each other I'm sure plus the way she instantly hugged Marley on arrival.

After the embrace, Chang made his way over to Dave and reminded him, "Ten minutes to go, Mr Dave," he said in Broken English.

"Right. I'm off to the light the flares, so your boss can land his helicopter John."

Dave finished speaking and exited the room through the same door he had entered. Then, Chang told us four of our rooms were ready if we would like to freshen up before the meeting started.

Food was also to be laid on in the form of a buffet

at 22.30 hours. We all started to make our way up the oak staircase. Tanya and Arthur went first and I followed with John, who was enquiring as to what I had been up to.

"Not much really, mate. Normal life I guess. Until my wife decided she wanted to be single again, which I must admit knocked me flat. (At this comment Tanya gave a glance my way.) Then, somehow fate grabbed me, shuck me up a little, and here I am." I told him.

I asked John if he was still in the SAS.

"Sort of," he replied.

"And, don't tell me. Tanya is a member of the SAS as well."

"No, Steve. Tanya is like what Arthur said. She's the Brigadiers PA, and for that role she has to be a serving police officer," John informed me.

"Who's the Brigadier then?" I asked then said sorry for been nosy,

"Charles Howlett," replied John, "You ask what you want. I will help if I can. You have a lot of catching up to do." He informed me.

Just as we got to the top of the stair case Arthur prompted me to follow him, "This way, Steve."

I followed, but felt compelled after a few paces to glance at Tanya. I kept walking, but looked backwards at her. At the same time she was glancing in my direction. I got embarrassed and quickly looked front again.

22.10 Hours

I HAD JUST laid on top of the great four poster bed after showering and inspecting the adjoining the room. Just like the rest of the place, it had been designed impeccably.

In the corner was a spa bath with twelve water jets. The walls around the bath and the ceiling above were all totally mirrored with the remaining walls and ceilings encased with beautiful marble tile. The floor was also marble, but it was several shades darker.

The bath, basin, and other facilities were porcelain with brass/gold fittings. As you walked back into the bed room, your feet were supported on a flush carpet like I had never seen.

Laying there on the soft bed, I had just closed my eyes and was very nearly asleep, when I heard a knock on the door. "Come in," I shouted.

Arthur entered. "What do you think about the room then?"

Throwing my feet off the bed and onto the lush carpet again I replied, "It just gets better and better."

Arthur made his way over to what looked like a small antique chest of drawers and bent down asking me if I would like a drink.

"Drink?"

I looked where he was and wondered why he had even asked. Then I said, "Yes please. A beer or lager."

He pulled open the front of the chest of drawers, (which was fake) and inside it was a mini bar. Arthur passed me a Budweiser and took a small Bells Whiskey for himself. He poured the Bell's into a glass and dropping a couple of ice cubes on top. Before he took a sip, he pushed the glass arm's length to me saying, "Cheers."

I tapped his glass with my bottle replying, "Cheers, Arthur."

AT THAT MOMENT, I knew my life had changed forever.

22.27 Hours

WE WALKED INTO the conservatory, and Chang swiftly brought over a tray of drinks. Still with my bottle half full, I declined. However, Arthur relieved him of two glasses. Shortly after being joined by John and Tanya, we made our way over to the left hand side of the conservatory where Chang and Marley were uncovering the buffet… and what a buffet it was. I was just about to grab a plate and tuck in when Dave, Sarah and a very smart, tall gentleman entered.

John and Tanya immediately said, "Good evening, sir."

"Evening," replied the Brigadier.

Dave then introduced me.

"Good evening, sir." I said, as if I were back in the army.

The Brigadier replied, "Always good to meet a new member of Dave's outfit." At that, he put out his hand for me to shake. Then he continued, "You must be something special to be brought in on one of my operations son at such short notice. But, Dave knows what he is doing."

The brigadier finished shaking my hand, and then turned to Marley saying, "I am looking forward to tasting your delicious food, Marley."

She smiled and slightly bowed again informing Charles he was always welcome to enjoy her food.

Turning now to Arthur he said, "And, how are you Arthur?" the Brigadier questioned.

"I'm fine, as always. You know me Charles. One of life's rolling pennies."

The Brigadier cut Arthur off sharply and returned with,

"I'm glad to hear that, because I think you will be interested in someone who will be mentioned in tonight's briefing."

The Brigadier then made his way to the front of the conservatory and placed his brief case on a small table next to a lectern. Everything had been set out for him earlier. We all finished our food. Dave inquired if the Brigadier was ready to start.

"Yes Dave. If you all could be seated, we will proceed. There is a lot to get through and not a lot of time." Tanya then left the Brigadier and went to sit down.

"Lights!" Dave commanded, and Chang switched them off.

Cane chairs had been set out for us to sit on facing the Brigadier. He set up his laptop computer and projected pictures on the wall/ screen.

I was sitting in the middle of Arthur and Tanya, when Tanya's scent surrounded me. Her perfume was faint but present.... I was entirely focused on her like a school boy, the screen popped up with a well-dressed man in his early fifties. Arthur seemed noticeably shocked to see this image.

The Brigadier began to speak. His voice was calm, but firm. He was conscious that he was not only talking to use, but remotely to several other members of Dave's company. Tanya had the desk set up with a Skype conference link.

"I know some of you will know this man." He gave an anguished glance at the photo.

Then he continued, "But for the ones that haven't had the delight of his company, his name is Harold Fletchly. Well, that's the alias he is using at the moment. Our intelligence service has at least six aliases on file for him. I am sure Arthur will be able to tell you the last one he used." The Brigadier stopped.

"Derrick Thornley!!" shouted Arthur, with a disturbing amount of hate in his tone.

The Brigadier resumed talking, himself also in a different tone now. He didn't appear to be as hateful as Arthur sounded, but there was a definite amount of disgust in his voice. The screen changed to a picture of a young attractive blonde girl.

"This young lady is the reason why this briefing is taking place this evening. Our friend Fletchly is back in our country." He had a sip of his drink. "As we sit here now, he's up in Scotland restocking his cult, and unfortunately, he is breaking no laws."

The Brigadier paused for a moment in both posture and speech. He needed a moment to collect himself... to get rid of his own personal sentiment and hate before continuing.

"This is Harold's next victim." He used a pen to highlight the photo of the girl. "This will be a big catch for Fletchly and the 'Lambs of God' as his cult is known. Her name is Susannah Kavanagh, and she is about to become the heiress to a personal fortune of 6.7 million pounds sterling, plus estate assets of 7.8 million."

As he said the amounts, several different photos appeared showing a stately home and surrounding land.

"Arthur and I know from past experience that as soon as Susannah has finished tying up all the loose ends of her fortune, she will then hand it over to the Lambs of God. A number of offerings to God will also appear to take place. Or should we say... several suicides will be arranged, or some other despicable act... rendering Susannah helpless."

The Brigadier was interrupted by Arthur shouting, "I know one suicide I would like to arrange." Arthur then shuffled in his chair and made his apologies to the Brigadier.

The Brigadier after acknowledging Arthurs hate and frustration, continued and clicked his remote control.

The picture changed again, and this time the image was of a burnt out building. At a guess, I would have said church or monastery. The Brigadier flicked again and the same image was magnified. The picture continued to get closer... again and again, until the camera man must have gotten as close as he dared. Now the image was much clearer. Visible on this last devastating picture was the charred remains of a group of a human corpses... burnt bones, some part covered with the remains of cooked flesh. One of the corpses was holding something. As I stared at this latest photo, I thought it looked as if this individual was trying to protect this object.

Then it fucking hit me like a tonne weight, and I mean made me feel physically sick. Yet, angry... wanting to tear the person responsible apart. The corpse was holding an infant... a BABY. I was devastated, tears filling my eyes. The photo stunned me... not letting me look away. It lured me in, the emotion provoking content was real, yet somehow my brain tried to convince me it wasn't real, trying to protect my sanity. The black charcoal bodies were all touching, as if they had huddled together to die.

The body was burned beyond recognition as it cradled the infant. It actually appeared, in some minute reassuring way, to be smiling, with still perfect teeth. At this point, my eyes allowed the rest of the frame to come into focus.

In the room were dozens of destroyed bits of furniture, smoke damaged paintings on the walls, and cracked widows. And strangely, there was a statue of the Virgin Mary... blindfolded.

All of a sudden the glamour and excitement of the last few days had become real and insignificant to what was on that screen. Arthur then got up and left the room.

The Brigadier clicked his button once more, and on the screen appeared a picture of a newspaper headline describing the scene: thirty-one men, women, and children had died... burnt to death in this mass suicide. The Brigadier left the image of the paper clipping on the wall and excited the room.

Dave stood up and asked Chang to switch on the lights, and then turned back to us and said, "I think this may be a good time for a break, help yourself to the buffet again and refresh your drinks." He then said a similar message into the skype.

The atmosphere in the conservatory was solemn.

I stood at the buffet table next to Dave and asked, "What is up with Arthur? I know those pictures were horrific and upsetting, but I would not have expected him to react like that?"

Dave came back with, "I think it's about time I came clean with you, Steve." And he took a drink, "Arthur's more upset than the rest of us, because he was sent to Germany by me on behalf of the British Government. He was to execute Harold Fletchly or Derrick Thornley as he was called then. However, he failed. He was found about twenty miles from that building you saw on those pictures he had been stabbed several times, knocked out, tied up and a note was left pinned to him saying.

"*Failed gain, Authority.*" It took weeks for Arthur to be well enough to just get out of hospital and then maybe a year before he returned to work."

I tried to ask a question but Dave just continued. "You see, Steve, Arthur had infiltrated the Lambs of God over there in Germany, and he was of the belief he could have saved all them people."

Just then Arthur and the Brigadier returned through the door and came towards us.

"Tanya pass me a clean glass for Arthur please."

After she did, I quickly filled it with Teachers whiskey. After what Dave had just told me I should have passed him the bottle.

"Cheers, Steve," said Arthur as he put a bundle of A4 sheets into his left hand leaving his right free to take the glass of me.

The Brigadier started talking to Dave, Sahara, John and Tanya. I looked at Arthur sipping his whiskey and didn't really know what to say.

Then, Arthur broke the ice and said,

"Steve, we have got a lot to discuss after the briefing." Then he just picked up and started eating some Chinese spring rolls. Dave asked us asked us if were ready to get back to the brief.

"Yes, of course," replied Arthur.

We followed the rest to regain our seats. Tanya reset the Skype connection then re-joined us. The Brigadier pressed his switch and the screen was blank.

Looking directly at all of us he spoke firmly and with conviction. "I make no apology for showing you those pictures. I needed to get across the evil we are dealing with."

The Brigadier touched his laptop and a computerized agenda was now on the screen. He then touched the third word down, more photos and another photo appeared. This one was of a girl around twelve with a man and a woman in their mid-thirties.

"This is Susannah at the age of thirteen with her parents. The parents were tragically killed in a light aircraft accident three years after this picture was taken."

He pressed his thumb against the screen now showing Susannah with two people in their fifties standing in front of a magnificent castle/stately home.

Brigadier continued, "This photo is the most recent of Susannah with her grandparents outside the Kavanagh's family house in Scotland. Susannah is eighteen here," he pressed the screen again. The next picture was of a dark haired young lady of a similar age, with a black eye, cut mouth and severely bruised cheek bone. The Brigadier pressed again and the photo enlarged.

"This is Abigail. She is also eighteen years of age, however this picture was taken by me yesterday in Scotland." There was movement at this from Tanya.

"You see, Abigail is or should I say *was*, Susannah's best friend. But instead of sharing every moment those young ladies do at their age, the last three months Abigail has struggled to even be able to talk properly with Susannah because of *this man.*"

The Brigadier changed the picture again to a long

distanced photo of Susannah and a young man of around eighteen to twenty years old. The Brigadier then went on to explain that the photo had been taken by Susannah's grandmother about six months ago. When this young man first started to appear on the scene, at first Susannah's grandparents were pleased. Kieran (*that's what the young man was called*) appeared to be a well-educated pleasant person and according to Susannah's grandmother, Susannah was genuinely happy.

However, it was Abigail who for the last three months had started to see the changes occurring in her friend. She decided to at last have it out with her.

It had been over a week since Abigail had spoken with Susannah. She waited for her friend to come out of her college room, and she was alone for once, no Kieran.

"Susannah," shouted Abigail.

"What's up? Why have you come looking for me?" snapped Susannah.

"We haven't spoken properly for nearly two weeks, and I haven't seen you at all this week. I am wondering what I have done to upset you?"

Abbey had to stop talking as she was trying hard to fight back her tears, but Susannah said nothing. She just starred at her watch and looked at the halls main door.

"Look, Susannah. We've been friends since we were six years old. You just can't cut me out like this without an explanation," said Abbey, now really shouting. With frustration.

Just then Susannah pushed right through Abbey, nearly knocking her shoulders off. Abbey turned and Kieran was standing with the hall door open with three or four of his zombies behind him like a posse. Abbey decided to have one last try and ran in front of Susannah, placing her hands on her shoulders to slow her down.

"Susannah, if our friendship is over, please come to my flat tonight. Tell me and you can pick up your belongings. If that's what you want," demanded Abbey.

She then stepped out of Susannah's way. Suddenly, to Abbey's astonishment, Susannah spun around and shouted, "Fine! I will be there at 6." Then she was off again.

On the way back to her flat Abbey was contemplating whether or not to ring Susannah's grandparents, so they could come and help her with convincing Susannah something had changed within her.

However Abbey was frightened it was drugs that had made these changes to her friend's personality and if that was the case she thought it best to find out for sure before telling the Kavanagh's as they would be devastated.

6.20 p.m. – No sign of Susannah.

ABBEY POURED HERSELF another glass of wine and had just put it to her lips when the doorbell rang.

She slammed her glass on the breakfast bar spilling

the wine everywhere and ran to the door. Full of hope that this would be an end to the stupid phase Susannah was going through.

"Come in," Abbey said joyfully as she threw open the door. She then tried to give her friend a hug which was perfectly normal for these two, but Susannah just pushed by Abbey and stormed into the kitchen.

"I hope you have something important to say to me. I've put things off to come here and I will only be here half an hour. Kieran is picking me up at 7:00 p.m."

Not even looking at Abbey, Susannah sat on a stool at the breakfast bar. Abbey felt sick and was upset by Susannah's outburst.

"Look, Susannah. I am worried about you and the way you are behaving." She then switched the kettle on but when she turned around again, Susannah was stood there right in her face.

"You're just jealous because I've got on with my life and you haven't. You used me when my parents died!" screamed Susannah.

With that Abbey swung out and hit Susannah across the face with everything she had. "I'm sorry! I'm sorry!" blurted out Abbey.

It was too late Susannah had fallen to the floor, as Abbey tried to reach for her to help her up. Susannah shuffled backwards to the kitchen door on her hands and flats of her feet. She then got up and ran for the front door. Abbey gave chase, but in vain because as she got to the door all she saw was Susannah running down the stone steps and into Kieran's arms.

Kieran was stood across the road in front of a racing green MG sports car. Abbey watched with tear filled eyes as Kieran walked her best friend around the MG and sat her in the front passenger seat.

He then walked back and glanced at Abbey with a sickening smile that said

'*Thanks, you've just clinched the deal for me*'. The MG sped off. Abbey walked back into her hallway, shutting the front door, which now had a crack in one of the glass panels due to the force of which Susannah slammed it.

Still not fully understanding what was happening, Abbey fell back against the wall and slumped to the floor. She was no longer able to hold back the tears and emotions she just burst out crying, and fell asleep.

9.20pm

ABIGAIL AWOKE CURLED up in a ball on the hall floor her blouse soaked with tears. She was not quite awake, and she thought she heard knocking on the door. The moon was full, and her eyes still moist with all the crying. She looked up to see a silhouette of a person behind the glass of the door.

Abbey stood up and she began to hope it was Susannah coming back to make up. On opening the door instead of it being her best friend it was Kieran.

"Susannah is very upset and has asked for me to come and speak to you." Kieran said.

Detecting no malice in his voice she let him in and

she made her way to the kitchen and Kieran followed.

"Where is Susannah staying? Have you taken her home? I'll ring her," Abbey asked Kieran.

"Susannah has instructed me to tell you she has no wish to see you again or her grandparents. She also believes she has found a place in our church The Lambs of God. For the first time since the death of her parents, she feels fully at peace with herself. She has found new friends and family within our church. Susannah sees her self been a member of our family for the rest of her natural life and her forth coming illuminated existence. She has no wish from this earth moment onwards to have any communication or contact with any person or persons from her former life. Any necessary communications Susannah feels must be made will be via one of our churches legal representatives." Kieran kept reading this message which seemed to be written on a medieval type scroll.

Abbey kept trying to interrupt saying, "What do you mean she doesn't want to see anybody and what's this Lambs of God thing? This church… this illumination?"

Kieran didn't answer. He didn't look away from the scroll. He just kept on reading. "Over the last few months, she has been a visitor to our church. She has now realised there is more to life then statues and wealth. Susannah now sees the possibility of sharing her forth coming inheritance to enhance the lives and wellbeing of others she now has contact with."

Abbey tried again to interrupt Kieran by saying,

"How many months has she been going to your church? It explains a lot; all the changes in her and me lying to cover were she is to her grandparents."

Kieran finished reading and then rolled the scroll up, placed it on the breakfast bar and then reached into his pocket to retrieve a pair of black leather driving gloves.

He slowly pulled the gloves onto his bony hands as he walked over to Abbey. She started to feel uneasy and frightened, Abbey tried backing away.

"There's no need to be scared. We need you alive to deliver this message," he said.

He was right up to her by now, and then from nowhere Kieran punched Abbey really hard, smacking her right on the cheek and nose.

Then, he calmly walked away saying, "I enjoy hurting women and you would do well to remember that before you decide to start interfering with our church." Kieran had a sinister smile on his face. He was nearly out of the kitchen when he turned and he looked right into her soul and said, "If you do decide to interfere with us, I look forward to hurting you Abigail."

Abbey was just standing there frozen to the spot, terrified, and shocked. She had never been hit before in her whole life, not even a tap off her parents. Her nose was bleeding, her ears ringing and stars were floating around in her eyes.

She heard the front door slam, but she didn't dare move. She just stood there feeling nauseous, from fear and the smell of Kieran's breath. Still frozen to the spot, Abby felt the blood running down from her nose over her lips and down her cheek. After a few minutes, Abby wiped her chin. She then found the courage to see if the coast was clear. She made for the hallway. The front door was open, but there was no sign of Kieran. She ran the full length of the hallway and straight out and down the worn smooth stone steps. Luckily living on the main street in the town there was always a taxi driving by.

"Taxi!" Abbey shouted really loud and waved her hand so she didn't miss it. The black London style cab shot over to her and pulled up outside Abbey's door. As the Taxi driver lit the orange in service light, Abby requested he waited.

"Just two minutes." She told the old pleasant look-ing cab driver.

She muttered to herself be strong, '*Come on… be strong.*' She had just remembered the scroll on the breakfast bar. So, off she ran for it, not stopping once up the steps through the hall. She grabbed the scroll and out again slamming the door shut on the way out. When she got in the taxi, the driver turned around to see where she wanted to go and noticed the state of Abbey's face.

"Are you alright Miss? Do you want to go the Hospital?" he asked sympathetically.

"No! Just take me to Kavanagh house, and quickly. Please," returned Abby as she sat back in the chair.

"Yes. Okay," he replied as he pulled out, completed a u-turned and shot off.

Abigail Connelly lived on her own because early that year her mother, father, and younger brother had moved to London on business. Because of College and her friends, Abbey stayed behind. However, Susannah's grandparents had promised to look out for her and they did. She was like a member of their family.

"We are here, Miss," said the taxi driver as they turned onto the gravel drive.

"Whereabouts would you like to be?"

"Straight to the main door, please," Abbey answered his question with,

"I will be one minute. Wait here," she said.

She left the cab, ran across the gravel to the main door as the driver watched. Instead of knocking on the main door or ringing the front bell, Abbey leaned behind the left pillar, which looked pretty strange to the driver watching.

But unbeknown to him, behind the pillar was another bell of which the existence was only known to family members and a few very close friends. This extra bell was in some way a code and gave the family some idea who would be calling.

Just then as Abby returned to the door, Diana the housekeeper opened the door,

"Hello, Abigail. Susannah is out if you are looking for her." Then, Diane noticed the state of Abbey's face.

"My God child! Look at your face! Come in. Come in." Diana was frantic.

"No... No... No! Just the Colonel." Abby

couldn't get her words out properly. She was stuttering because her adrenaline was flowing due to the fear and in response… the fight or flight had kicked in powerful chemicals. Abigail then just burst into tears, probably because she now felt safe again.

Diana ran across the entrance hall and knocked and opened a large internal door which led into the drawing room.

"Colonel its, Abbey! Come quickly please!" pleaded Diana.

When the Colonel saw Abbey's face he couldn't believe it.

"What has happened? Where is Susannah? Where have you been?" the Colonel asked.

"Diana, go and find Annabelle!"

Abbey then pointed outside and said,

"I've no money for the Taxi." Sir.

"Don't worry Abby," and the Colonel went to the main doors went through one of them and took his wallet out as he approached the taxi,

"How much my good man?" asked the Colonel.

"£6.50 please, sir," replied the cabby.

The Colonel passed him £10 telling him to keep the change and also apologised for him having to wait. The driver then enquired if the young lady was ok. The Colonel thinking fast on his feet trying to do a damage limitation exercise said,

"She will be fine. We've just sent for the Doctor. She is a friend of my granddaughter and has just had a bad accident playing hockey."

"Please give her my best," said the driver and he drove off, slowly crunching the gravel under tire.

The Colonel then returned to the house to find Annabel, Susannah's grandmother, and Diana fussing around Abbey. She had now calmed down, enough to start explaining what was happening.

"Let us go into the drawing room. Diana, will you please make Abbey a pot of tea and draw her a hot bath with plenty of my lavender salts?" asked Annabelle smiling at Abbey.

Annabelle and the Colonel then supported Abby into the drawing room where she started to explain what had been happening over the last few months to result in this evening's episode.

"Three months! Susannah has been telling us that she was spending four nights at your apartment every week. That you were both revising together," said a surprised Annabelle.

"She has not spent a night at my flat for at least four months. This last month I've hardly seen her anywhere. That is why I forced her to come and see me tonight." Abbey then passed the scroll to the Colonel. Annabelle and the Colonel looked at each other with a shock.

"Did Susannah do that to your face Abbey?" asked Annabelle.

"No, this was Kieran," Abbey gently touched the swelling on her cheek then continued.

"Yes, Kieran did it. He read that scroll to me. Told me Susannah never wanted to see me or anyone ever again from her former life including you two. He then put his gloves on and punched me. He left the scroll and went. That's why I had to come here. I was so frightened not just for me but for Susannah he told me he enjoyed hurting women," she told them with fear in her voice.

Annabelle put her arm around Abbey who had started to cry again, crying more for Susannah this time than herself.

"Just one more question my dear. Who are these Lambs of God?" asked the Colonel.

"All I know, sir, is there are a few of these silly churches that are always trying to get you to attend their meetings," answered Abbey, who then took a small sip of tea the cup shuck in her hands as she did so.

The Colonel was clearly angry, and started to organise.

"Diane, you make sure Abbey gets her bath. Annabelle will you see if it's possible for the Doctor to come and take a look at Abbey?" Finishing speaking, the Colonel got up and made his way to his study to contact the Police.

The Colonel now sitting at his desk picked up the phone and started to dial, but then replaced the receiver. He then rolled open the scroll and put a paper weight top and bottom and read it again. 'Right, Simon,' he said to himself and re-dialled. After explaining what had happened to his granddaughter and to Abbey, the Sergeant assured the Colonel someone from CID would be with him within the hour. Just after he had put the receiver down again, the study door opened and Annabelle was stood there.

"Simon, what are we to do?" Annabelle's voice was full of despair.

Simon spoke.

"I don't know yet Annabelle, let's wait and see what the Police have to say this could all be a flash in the pan and may be over tonight. In the meantime, we must be strong for Abbey as well as Susannah. Anna love why don't you go and see how Abbey is doing. The Doctor must be here by now." Simon gave Annabelle a hug and a peck on the cheek.

"I will," replied an emotional Annabelle.

The Colonel sat back down and began reading the scroll again, but still made no sense of it. It seemed to be a number of mixed up sentences written in old English and maybe a bit of French and German.

The detail involved in making the scroll was excellent. It must have taken hours, if not days, to do all these scribed pictures and letters. To the Colonel this made it more sinister. The most worrying aspect was at the bottom… where you would expect to find a signature, there were four thumb prints in blood along with some human hair that had been woven into the paper itself.

There was then another knock at the door.

"Come in," shouted the Colonel.

Diane entered and announced, "The Police have arrived, sir."

"Show them in, please," the Colonel replied. She opened the study door fully and asked the gentleman to go in. The two men entered.

"Good evening, sir. I am Sergeant Wilson and this is my colleague Detective Constable O'Connor," the sergeant said.

The Sergeant was wearing a smart dark suit. But the Constable had slacks on and a rugby shirt and was unshaven. Both of the men took out their wallets to show the Colonel their ID's.

The Constable then made a quick apology for his dress, explaining he had just been involved in some close surveillance work. The Colonel asked the gentlemen to be seated.

"Not a problem. Your clothes are not important right now. I just want my granddaughter back as soon as possible," the Colonel commanded sitting back down.

Diane was still stood at the study door when she asked, "Will that be all for now sir?"

"No would you please let my wife know that the Police are here, and also bring some coffee please, Diane," instructed the Colonel.

"Of course sir." She closed the door and went to carry out her duties.

"Right, sir. We have only had a quick briefing over the telephone but when kidnap was mentioned, priority was given to your case. If you would like to explain from the beginning," said the Sergeant as he and the Constable opened their note books.

The Colonel spoke, "If we could just wait a few more minutes for my wife, as I would like her to be here to make sure I don't miss anything out. You understand. Also will you require to see Abbey tonight? She is Susannah's friend. The one, who thank God, brought all of this to our attention. It's just that the Doctor is with her at the moment, and she is very shaken up," the colonel finished speaking.

"That's fine Colonel. We will let her get a good night's sleep and speak to her in the morning," answered the Constable.

Just then as the door opened and in walked Anna-belle.

"Sorry to have kept you waiting gentleman. I've just been up with the Doctor and Abbey. The good news is there is no concussion, and the bruising should be gone within the next seven days."

Diana followed Annabelle into the study carrying a silver tray of coffee which Annabelle took from her saying, "Thank you, Diana. If you could check on Abbey for us then that will be all for this evening."

"Of course Ma'am," and Diana closed the door.

The two Police Officers stood up as a form of courtesy. As Annabelle reached the desk putting down the tray she said, "Help yourselves to coffee," and she walked round the large desk to the Colonel's side.

The Colonel and his wife for the next thirty minutes told the Officers everything they knew. Even about the total surprise which hit them, when they found out of Susannah's involvement with this cult thing.

After taking notes the Sergeant then said, "Please

do not take what I am going to say the wrong way. But from what you have told us, there has been no law broken and no kidnap. The only crime at the moment is assault on Abbey."

The Sergeant finished, and Annabelle answered back in a slightly raised voice, "What are you suggesting, Officer?"

"Please, let me explain. I've had dealings with this cult before about five years ago. I had only just got into plain clothes, and we spent hundreds of man hours trying to rescue or should I say, trying to find a legal way of regaining the freedom of a well-respected clergymen's daughter. From the clutches of this evil cult, but to no avail. Luckily, for us an inspector from Scotland Yard was on holiday fishing here. He'd popped into our station to use our fax machine. By chance, he overheard our conversation about this cult. Within a day, three men, from I presume Scotland Yard, were down and had taken over the case."

Annabelle interrupted with, "Was the girl alright?"

"I believe so, but the family left the village. Apparently there is a special liaison unit based at Scotland Yard, which deals with these case type. It's made up of police, army and civilian units. I've still kept the name and number. I will contact them first thing in the morning, and I am sure they will be in touch with you immediately."

The Sergeant finished with, "Any more questions Sir, Ma'am? Before we leave you."

"Yes," said the Colonel.

"What happened to this Lambs of God thing after Scotland Yard had dealings with them?"

"Well, we know they got the girl out. Then for about six months after that, we made their lives a misery where we could, within the law, and most of them seemed to disappear. They still have property here and hold the odd meeting. But, for the past four years, really not a murmur out of them until tonight that is."

"Thank you, Officers for your time and under-standing," the Colonel said as he rose from his chair.

"I'll show you out." And he led them outside.

Standing next to the four stone pillars outside the great house, the Colonel shook both of the Officer's hands.

"I'll be in touch with the yard first thing, but please feel free to contact me if you haven't heard anything by ... shall we say 12.00 hours? Goodnight, Colonel." The Sergeant joined his colleague in the car and they drove off.

The Colonel closed and locked the large door as he returned inside. Annabelle had heard Simon come back in and came through to meet him in the hall. They both returned to the drawing room for a well-earned night cap. The splendour and unique design of the room had been constructed over four centuries by different members of the Kavanagh family, yet every piece of furniture and antique matched the divine decoration.

Simon wearing a quality cotton, white shirt with a

dark intermittent thread running through it, turning the shirt checked, with light red canvas trousers secured with a soft brown leather belt and house shoes.

Simon now standing at the drinks trolley removing the stopper from the hand cut crystal decanter, pouring himself and Annabelle a whisky (ice in his and water in Annabelle's). Annabel who was slightly bending down over the open fire, breaking open the blackened red embers with a large ornate brass and ivory poker.

She was dressed in quality black slacks which covered the tops of her plain but beautiful black leather boots with a beige large interwoven jumper and an oversized polo neck collar with a large opening. Her hair was in impeccably styled and finished with small sleeper gold ear rings. The following morning after breakfast, Mrs Kavanagh set out to chair a WRVS meeting where she was to speak about the modern women's roll in today's world.

During breakfast the Colonel and Annabelle had decided to carry on as normal, and they asked Diana to remain silent for the moment which was really a formality. Diana was a fifty-three year old spinster who had been the aid and housekeeper for the Kavanagh family for thirty-three years and was devoted to them. In fact I would have liked to see the SS try and get information out of Diana.

11.10 a.m.

THE COLONEL HAD just returned from walking the dogs and was just hanging up his tweed shooting jacket in the back entrance next to the kitchen when Diana walked in.

They both spoke together and Diana stopped saying, "Please carry on, Colonel."

"I was just going to inquire if Abbey was awake and how she was?"

"Yes, I've just been up with a sandwich and a cup of tea and told her not to worry."

"Thank you, Diana. Any other messages?" asked the Colonel

"Yes, sir. Inspector McPherson has called from Scotland Yard and left a mobile number which he asked if you could call him on." Diane walked to the Colonel and handed him the note paper which she had wrote the number down on.

"Thank you. Are you alright with all this Diana?" Simon asked her.

"Yes Colonel. Worried, of course, but I'm sure all will work out for the best," answered Diana.

"I am sure your correct Diana. We really do take you for granted sometimes. You are such a pillar of strength to us," spoke Simon, with true genuine sentiment in his voice.

"I will be in my study if I'm required, Diana," and he finished taking off his wellingtons and put on a pair of house shoes. Going through the kitchen to his study, he grabbed a glass of fresh orange juice. Diane made a point to leave him a glass in that very spot at the same time every day for him when he returns from his walk.

After the Colonel had left, Diana placed the kettle

on the arga oven to bring to a boil and started to prepare the Colonel's lunch tray. As she was busy doing this, she said out loud a short prayer, 'Please, God, let Susannah be returned to us safe and sound and may the family be happy again, Amen'.

The Colonel was sitting at his desk and had just dialled the last two digits of the mobile number. It rang twice and he heard, "Stuart McPherson."

"Could I speak to Inspector McPherson?"

"Speaking," replied Stuart

"Inspector, this is Colonel Kavanagh."

"Ah, Colonel. Thank you for getting back to me. And please Sir, call me Stuart. I am on my way to see you now. I should be with you around 16.00 hours. If you could recommend a decent place to stay…"

The Colonel butted in with, "Nonsense, Inspector. Sorry, Stuart. You will be our guest. I insist."

"That will be great. Have you had any further contact from the cult or your granddaughter Colonel?" asked Stuart.

"No… Nothing, Stewart," Simon replied.

"Whatever you feel like doing… don't make contact yourself. I will see you later today. Goodbye for now Colonel," Stuart told him as he hung up his phone. Suddenly, there was a knock on the study door.

"Come in," spoke the Colonel.

"Good morning, sir," Abbey said.

"Come in girl. Take a seat. How are you?" genuinely enquired the Colonel.

Abbey still in her pyjamas and dressing gown hair

tied back, replied, "I feel a little better today. Is there any news about Susannah?"

"Yes, sort of. I've just put the phone down after speaking to an Inspector at Scotland Yard. He is on his way, and he is staying here tonight," replied Simon.

The phone then began to ring again.

"This will be Annabelle," Said the Colonel. He picked up the receiver again saying, "Hello… Colonel Kavanagh."

"Simon is that you?" a voice questioned.

"Who is this?" The Colonel enquired unable to recognise the voice.

"It's Charles. Charles Howlet. How are you Simon?"

"Charles, bloody good to hear your voice. I didn't recognise your voice at first."

"No you wouldn't Simon, as I am on my hands free mobile speaker. Damn technology you just can't escape it these days. Anyway, I will cut straight to the point Simon. I'm on my way to see you," said Charles.

"To see me? Why are in you in the area?" the Colonel replied surprised to be speaking to his friend as it had been 7-8 years since they had last spoken.

"No, Charles. I have just left Cambridge, and I'm meeting Stuart McPherson in Edinburgh. He is part of my team on cases of this nature, and when I received the fax this morning with the Kavanagh name on it, especially Susannah, I had to deal with this one personally. I will fill you in on all the details later, I just wanted to call and I will see you tonight," said Charles.

"You will stay with us of course," the Colonel came back with.

"Most definitely! I am sure you will have some decent whiskey, and pass my regards onto Annabelle." And Charles was gone.

"Well, that's two guests tonight Abbey. We had better inform Diana," the Colonel spoke as they both left the study together.

South Armagh, Northern Ireland 1986 – 11.00 hrs.

OUR BRICK RESUMED patrol. The destination was an old disused border patrol box about ten miles away across some rough terrain. We were aiming to arrive at the border box at around 14.00 hours. This box was located ½ a click on our side of the border making this a very dangerous place. (click = mile)

It would take them an hour to safely rekey the box, and another hour, at least, to complete a full search of it. (Mistakes were not an option, not if we all wanted to go home.) In N. Ireland the biggest killer of British Soldiers was booby traps or IED's Improvised Explosive Device. (As you may have heard in the world news)

We had now covered approximately nine of the ten mile patrol, but had used virtually our full three hours allotted due to the terrain which was just about straight up the side of a mountain. (Felt like a goat)

Just as we reached a plateau, Dave turned and signalled for Chris to join him. We all stopped. Chris skirmished his way to Dave. Bash and me got down and moved into the under growth for cover from any possible hostile eyes.

I could see Chris bending down in front of Dave. Dave opened Chris's Bergen and the radio was on top. Removing the hand set, he then began pressing the presell switch on the hand set Dave spoke clearly, "Delta 1, to Zero, Delta 1 to Zero are you receiving over?" Then he let go of presell switch.

"Zero receiving you Delta 1. Loud and clear. Send when ready over," replied Zero.

"Delta 1 all is fine on track as agreed over," Dave let go again of presell.

"Zero to Delta 1. Message received and understood. Zero out," and the radio stopped crackling. Dave re-secured the radio by pulling the draw string to close up Chris's Bergen and then called for Bash to join him.

Bash arrived and I could see Dave's arm stretched, fully pointing something out to them both. Next, they were going down the mountain. Dave signalled for me to join him. I got there and I knelt down with him. He pointed out the border box, which you could make out at the bottom of the valley.

Only about 1/4 of a click away and this last leg was downhill. (*Relief*)

Dave then pointed out Bash and Chris. They both had moved into a small clearing in a secluded area which was on the edge of a flat cliff about two hundred and fifty meters from Dave and me. I could just make out Basher sighting his GPMG in the direction of our target the border box. Dave then passed me his binoculars and pointed to a large tree passed the two of them.

We would position ourselves there and give cover, whilst Bash and Chris got safely into their next position. There they would eventually give us covering fire if we needed it as we made entry.

The plan was to move into the box in four stages. The final one being Dave and me with our knives out, on all fours looking for IED snares. Just then, Chris waved to us meaning they were in a spot to cover our move.

Dave turned to me and said, "5 meter gap Steve, and keep rotating for rear protection as we are going to be really vulnerable on this last stretch."

The following stage to the tree trunk took next to no time. We virtually followed an old shepherds trail. Before we knew anything, we were on the last stage approximately twenty meters away from our target.

Dave and I kept on stag whilst Chris and Bash moved into a clump of bushes and camouflaged up. They were going to be there for at least an hour and half maybe longer. If they were seen, Dave and I would be fucked as well. Because at that point we would be crawling to the box on all fours with our knives out, and our gats slung on our backs. If there was an attack this would be the equivalent of been caught with your pants down.

It had just started to rain when Basher crept up. "Alright Steve?" he asked.

"Yes, Bash. What's happening?" I replied.

"Go and get a quick coffee with Dave in our den before you go booby trap hunting." Bash whispered.

I shuffled backwards of the ledge I was on, and then removed the branches and bits of moss from my back and head giving them to Bash for his camouflage. I crawled about another fifteen feet just past an opening then got up and made my way to Bash's den. (Sounds like a name for an old East End boozer!)

I just got there and Chris was coming out of the entrance, "Alright, Steve. There's a pot of coffee made for you in there, but don't spill it on my carpet." He smiled and went off to relieve Dave.

17.15 Hours

WE HAD SUCCESSFULLY taken over the border box and just finishing our tea. (*Dried fruit biscuits and a protein shake*)

Dave was on the radio requesting to speak to Captain Jones, "Zero to Delta 1. Are you receiving? Over."

"Delta 1, receiving you. Send. Over."

"Inform Captain Jones from Delta 1, the weather is still fine? We will send you a coded message and would like a reply in the same format within thirty minutes. Over," clearly spoke Dave.

"Roger that. Zero send now. Over."

Dave started to relay a load of numbers and letters down the radio. This would just sound like a load of gibberish to anyone else listening in on our frequency.

But to Zero, they would place these numbers alongside today's graph and make sense of the message. (Can't explain any more you understand) Twenty minutes had passed and we received a message back from zero. Dave got his code book out and started to decipher our reply.

"It's all go men. We have the green light." Dave was totally excited.

Basically, Dave had sent a message to say we were going to cross the border tonight at 22.00 hours, and it would take us two hours to find and check the old barn which was our next objective.

Zero had then come back with, "Fine and be careful, and if we haven't heard from you by 00.00 hours we will commence evasive action. Out."

The next two hours, we just laid up resting, cleaning weapons and finalising maps. Tonight's mission was already getting our blood stirring. After all, this was bandit country and patrols of the IRA had been seen here in numbers of 10-12 men. Which would mean a serious fire fight for us, and probably an escape and evasion job. John had also said to Dave on the way out that he believed if any were Mr. X would be in this barn if he was still alive.

(*This I can appreciate may sound exciting to you, but believe me you are literally running and hiding for your life. Four soldiers against twelve trained and ruthless IRA, and we would also be well out gunned. Then, if you're caught, you fight and really fight because if they would take you, you're fucked. There have been cases of squaddies, been torn limb from limb. None of this ever got into the news as the powers to be never allowed it as the people of Northern Ireland including the IRA were British. So this would not have gone down well.)*

I had just finished checking my first aid equipment, of which I had a hell of lot more than usual. John had given me a full SAS field pack just in case Mr X was seriously injured, plus the reserve pack Dave had arranged. Looking up and across at Bash, he was sat there stroking a sharpening block up and down his ten inch hunting knife. Dave was laid on his back resting his eye lids and Chris was out on stag. (Duty)

The rain now had been falling hard over an hour the norm really for Ireland, yet still it was a lovely night with a full moon. Because we were not familiar with the territory we were in, plus the moon light would help us spot any patrols at a good distance. I then told myself to rest my eyes so I kipped (slept) for ten minutes. I thought of nothing apart from our forth coming entry into the barn which was not going to be conventional to say the least!

20.30 Hours

WE ALL CAME alive and started to prepare for the nights adventures.

"Cheers Dave," I said as he had just helped me on with my Bergen, which was now a lot heavier. As I would be the only one carrying a back pack tonight.

The other three lads would be just wearing the basics after stripping down to skeleton order. This was made up of magazine pouches, water bottle, knives, radio, in Chris's case, and weapons, of course. The reason for this was, if we got ambushed they would fight while I got to cover and removed the Bergen. We would not have stood a chance if we all had back packs on.

The rest of our gear was going to remain here. This however was a big no-no in N Ireland, because someone could put snares/ IED's on it. To combat this, we would, on our return, secure a ten meter rope to the gear and pull it. This would ensure that if it had been booby trapped it would blow up with us at a safe distance.

We knew what we were doing and we really had no other choice. If we did get ambushed tonight, and with us been this close to the boarder, (there was a real chance of this happening) if we were all wearing Bergens, we would have no chance of surviving. Having 10 stone plus secured to your back does not allow you to move quickly. Believe me… we would have been like the Dodo's were when the sailors landed. At least with three of us in fighting order, the brick had a chance.

22.10 Hours

WE SPOTTED THE barn. It was well lit in the moon-light, staying back at a distance of seven hundred to eight hundred meters. We grouped up in some cover.

I took off the Bergen (*thank fuck, it was heavy!*). Dave pointed to a couple of spots where we could observe for thirty minutes, and in this bright light anyone around the barn would have stood out like a glow worm.

23.15 Hours

DAVE AND I moved into a distance from the barn of about one hundred meters. Then, Dave put his fingers over the red lens of his torch. Before turning it on, he lifted and pointed it in the direction of Bash and Chris. He proceeded to opened two of his fingers giving a signal.

We then received from them the same signal been flashed back, which informed us they were in position and ready to cover our entry. Dave put his torch away and gave me his rifle. I altered the straps and slung it over my back (now free of the Bergen). Dave checked his browning, and he asked me for the tin of lighter fluid.

"Careful with that. It's very flammable," I cautioned. "Have you got your matches?" I continued.

He tapped his breast pocket and nodded, and then he was gone. A zigzagged sprint to what looked like an old well, and from there to the corner of the barn. I could then see him squirting the lighter fluid on a couple of the rotten old boards. He took his matches out of his pocket. (*We always carried survival matches, which were really more like a little flare than a match. With ten times the amount of sulphur of a regular match and then coated in wax for water proofing.*)

Dave then struck one of these, instantly igniting the

lighter fluid. (*Fucking hell on earth it went up!*) Dave flew backwards falling on to his arse. Quickly getting up, he ran to the nearest wall.

We all then waited (*no sound, no movement*) for the allotted time three minutes as planned. (*A long time in these situations*)

Bash and Chris were now on their way down to where I was hidden. I watched like a sniper as they ran into my position, again always giving cover. The minute they arrived, just like an Olympic relay team, I was off.

Dave and I then ran straight to the fire with wet sand bags and our shovels. We managed quite quickly to put the fire out and then forced some boards off the side of the barn ready for our entry.

Inside the barn was exceptionally dark, but you could just make out objects and dimensions because of the moonlight which crept in between the old and missing boards. Before we entered, we glanced over and yes, there it was. A small red light which was our signal to say that Bash and Chris were fully in a position and covering us.

Just before we squeezed through the slot we had made, I started to laugh. Dave's eyebrows *were missing*!!

"It's not fucking funny," he said and pushed me against the barn, then he entered first (*It was funny. His face totally camouflaged with green, brown and black. Then there were these two bare skin and melted hair marks*). I passed through his rifle, followed then by mine. I squeezed through and joined him. It was a pretty large barn, twenty meters across and maybe fifteen meters deep. One side was open plan, just a couple of stone troughs on the floor and a number of big round poles holding up the roof. On the other side, there were four or five stable like cubicles. Which we could not see into, but the idea of the fire was to smoke out any rats! After all they didn't know we were going to put it out again so quickly.

Dave leaned over to my ear and whispered, "I'll check each one out with the torch. If anything happens, shoot the fuck out of the cubicle."

I slung his rifle over my back. He held out his browning pistol with the torch underneath in his left hand. Cautiously, he stepped towards the cubicles. *Torch on* first cubicle. *Torch off. Torch on* second cubicle. I kept my SA80 rifle on my shoulder and followed the cubicles down. I was so tensed up that I don't remember breathing. *Torch off. Torch on.* This time it stayed on. I kept my rifle shouldered and prowled up to Dave but keeping behind him. I got just up to him, and I could see his torch beam was fixed on what looked like a mass of rolled up Hessian sacks.

The trouble being that the amount there, was large enough to conceal a man/ body. Dave then shined his torch twice towards the two remaining cubicles. I automatically knew this meant to keep an eye here, but I'm going to check them last two. I knelt down keeping my sight trained on the pile of Hessian. The dark reappeared as Dave moved with his torch, yet with patches of moon light and given the fact my eyes were now in night mode, I would have noticed any movement. (*Little tip for you... in the dark, look just to the right of the object and the left eye picks it up much easier.*)

Both the remaining cubicles were empty. Dave came back to me and communicating in sign language, he made it clear he was going to go and investigate the pile of hessian. I remained knelt down.

My rifle now aimed where Dave's red spot pointed from his torch. Bent over, he pushed the pile of hessian with his browning first – nothing. He then leaned further in, to grab a handful and pulled. At that moment I said a silent prayer.

"Fucking hell," I said under my breath if this lot had been rigged with C4, we would be in bits. (*Just another day at the office*)

Out of the hessian sacks rolled a body covered in what looked like blood. Dave kicked it, no movement. Then, he knelt down to check for snares. Nothing found. He took the pulse.

He turned to me, "Not sure if he's alive... just check, Steve," he whispered.

I removed Dave's rifle and gave it to him with mine. I then looked the body fully over and tried the jugular in his neck for a pulse, but nothing. I shook my head to Dave, informing him no pulse. Yet there was something inside me said he is alive.

It looked like our Mr X from the description we had gotten from John. I had to try again. I unrolled my first aid tools. In the roll, there was a small mirror. I placed it just above the body's mouth and nostrils, and then counted to six. Holding the mirror at arm's length, I shone my torch onto it, and yes there was mist on the glass. He was breathing.

I turned to Dave and nodded my head then mimed, "He is breathing." A small smile appeared on Dave's hard face.

Now inspired with finding life, I went to work. Discovering his wounds were deep slashes to his upper left bicep, his knees had been drilled. The right one looked like the drill bit must have gotten stuck, and this ripped out his knee cap and the cartilage. He must have passed out at this... one small mercy.

On the front of his torso, there was a small bullet entry hole approximately 4/5 millimetres left of his chest towards his shoulder. Turning the body over, I noted that the bullet had exited, however it resembled a bag of butchers waste. (*How this virtual fluid less corps was alive, totally beyond me*)

"Dave," I whispered he bent over and took a look at his back.

"What the fuck? Can you do anything for him?" Dave came back with.

"I'll have to just get as many dressing's on as possible, stitch the bicep and cover with a field dressing. Then I will have to splint both legs together after bagging and taping the knees. His right arm is not a problem. A field dressing will do that. He is a fucking mess, Dave. I'm going to have to get an IV drip into him continually, but I just don't think I will get a line in to him. I'm going to have to do a Murthy drip."

"Through his arse you mean," commented Dave.

"Yes. At least for an hour to get some hydration in via his Colon, plus the speed of rehydration will be slow if we got a line in a vain we would bring is salt content up to quickly and this would thin his blood and could cause the brain to swell." I replied.

Dave then spoke saying "Fuck Steve you sound like a Doctor," He gave me an unenvied look. I took this to mean he also could smell the stench I was sucking in. The throat clogging aroma was an un-even mix of horse manure, blood starting to smell sweet as it began to rot, and the overpowering influx of human faeces that was hours old.

Looking at the feet attached to this man, someone had been electrocuting him with a battery charger. I knew this because of the burns, bruises, and the imprinted holes in the skin where the Crocodile clips had been applied. This was a common torture practice, and also made the recipient empty their bowls.

"With the amount of blood he has lost, I'm surprised he his alive!" I spoke but believed it as well.

"Right, Steve. I'll go to the main door and signal the other two. They will bring your Bergen with the first aid kit."

He put my rifle down next to me. After checking the door for booby traps, Dave opened one of the doors about six inches. As he looked out, Dave was just about to signal with his torch when he spotted Bash and Chris running down the hill towards him. Each of them holding a strap of my Bergen. When they got within twenty feet of the barn door, Dave pulled it open to approximately three feet, and then showed himself.

Both of them ran inside dropping the Bergen as they felt safe. Dave pushed the heavy door, the bottom of it dragged through the dirt. He shouldered into place the large wooded obstacle the final four inch. Then, he bent down and picked up the length of six by three timber. He dropped this back in the slots securing the massive door.

"What are you two playing at?" Dave demanded to know.

Out of breath Chris answered him, "Fucking hell, Dave give us a chance. There is a hostile patrol out there. At least eight with balaclavas with full combats and looked like they were carrying AK47's," Chris told him.

Then, Dave told Bash to give the Bergen to me and shone the torch in my cubicle.

"How far behind you were they?" Dave asked Chris.

"That last hill we came over tonight, we spotted their silhouettes coming over there," informed Chris. Then he spoke again, "I got the night scope out for a second look, and then I knew we had better warn you. They can't be more than ¼ of a click away." Chris finished the mini brief.

Dave put his arm around Chris and brought him over to me and Bash.

I'd just dressed the wounds and got an inflatable

splint on the legs. I tried in poor light to get a fluid drip into Mr X with no success, so I did as expected the Murthy drip. Bash passed me a litre of fluid and asked how he was doing.

"Well, I think we may have increased his pulse, and if we can get two of these litre solution into him over the next few hour or so, we might be able to keep him alive."

Then shaking my head I quietly announced to Bash, "I don't rate his chances." Bash then made the cross your heart sign.

"But no matter what he's going to have to be carried on a stretcher," I insisted.

"We've got about two minutes to get out of here Steve, and we haven't got stretcher," Dave told me.

"Why two minutes?" I asked surprised.

"Didn't you tell him, Bash?"

"No, he was busy…" Bash answered in his style.

"Steve there is an enemy patrol about five minutes away if we are lucky," Dave spitted out. He then looked at me and then at Mr X.

"Shit. They're coming back to make sure he's dead," I realised.

"It looks that way. Anybody got any brilliant ideas?" Dave asked as he was looking around the barn then at us.

The rain was back, but this wasn't the only noise outside we could hear rustling. Then, we heard a couple of weapons been cocked (*made ready to fire*). Dave and I covered Mr X up again with the Hessian bags.

Bash and Chris hid, but Dave and I were still in the cubicle. We watched as something was slipped between the gap in the doors, and this knocked the securing timber up and out of the hooks. The door was opened.

I jumped into the next cubicle just in time to see the moonlight enter the barn. As the door was pushed open wider, the light beam seemed to begin to search the whole barn. Luckily for us the heavy door wedged stuck at ninety degree angle to the cubicles. This meant the strip of light was six feet away from us.

As we hid, we heard in a strong Irish accent, "I'll see if the English scum is dead. You keep an eye out here."

Just as the beam of light was broken by the figure of this large man, I was crouched in the corner of the second cubicle.

He walked past me and then he switched a torch on. Then, I heard the Irish accent say, "Who the fuck are you?"

Dave must have still been in there because, the next thing I see is him walking past me, hands on the back of his head, and a rifle barrel stuck in his back. I still had Bash's hunting knife in my hand from cutting the bandage.

I got up and just shoved the knife straight through the man's neck, severing the larynx. Then, I twisted the jagged blade with the intension of this terrorist not being able to make a sound, instantly retracting the blade which caught on the spinal cord I could feel each of the knifes large teeth serrate on the muscle, cartridge and bone. I then caught him as he fell, his warm blood was pumping out all over me… the hot sticky fluid in my mouth, nostrils, ears, and running down my neck. Dave turned as I was dragging the body into the cubicle. He bent and picked up his feet, and we put the body in the corner.

Without even time to take a deep breath or say anything, another figure appeared in the doorway shouting, "Seamus are you there? Seamus?"

"Is he there?" a third Irish accent said from outside.

There were now two figures in the door way. I saw Dave reach inside his combat jacket and pull out his browning. 4 shots fired and both figures dropped.

"Basher close that fucking door!" shouted Dave.

The door was closed again. Nine seconds after Bash kicked the door shut, we all dropped like bags of spuds because at least ten fully automatic weapons opened fire on the barn. (*You're not alive until you have nearly died.*)

Bullet holes were appearing everywhere like little stars being born as the moonlight came through. Thousands of splinters of wood scattered everywhere. I rammed my face into the ground and put my hands on my head and just prayed. Then the firing stopped.

"Get behind those stone troughs," Dave shouted.

"I'll get Mr X," I told him and ran to the cubicle. I picked him up and then dumped him inside one of the troughs and dived behind it. Then, the barrage of bullets started again. I honestly thought the barn was going to collapse. There were that many holes now puncturing it.

"Everyone alright?" Dave shouted.

Chris said, "Yep."

Then I shouted, "Fine," but Bash didn't answer.

"Basher," Chris yelled, and I saw him try and get up.

"Get down you fucking idiot," Dave shouted.

It was a terrifying experience. You couldn't see the bullets, but I swear you could hear them flying above our heads. (*Yet also exhilarating you knew that you were alive, you just didn't know for how long*) Bits of stone were flying off the troughs. Dust, mud, and straw was falling on our heads, as was the rain now, because there were that many holes in the roof. The bullets stopped again.

Chris jumped up to check Bash.

"His head is bleeding and he's out cold!" Then, they started firing again. (*This is it!! I thought.*) Then, just then the sky truly lit up. This really bright light entered through the bullet holes like a second round. We had to cover our eyes. Then, I heard powerful machine gun fire almost definitely GPMP, followed by an explosion. Then silence. There was another burst of GPMG. The sound that followed that was the answer to our prayers.

It was the blades of a helicopter and then loud haler saying "Delta one. Are you ok?"

None of us said a word until we heard it again.

"Delta one, are you in there?" (*Oasis effect*)

Dave replied loudly this time with, "What is the colour of the day?" Each day we had a different colour for friendly forces identification.

"Today is white, but don't forget its gone 00.00 hours. Yesterday was yellow, that's what we are here for. You didn't send your last radio check." The voice was drowned out by the noise of a couple more helicopters. The dust was still flying around and large lumps of the roof were now falling in.

"I'll go first. Steve. Can you check Bash?" Dave got up dusted himself down and went towards the entrance.

Dave dragged the door open as I was feeling around, trying to clean and dress Basher's head. It was actually more of a graze than a cut. It looked like he must have knocked himself out as he dived to take cover over the trough. When he didn't answer during the cascade of bullets, we thought he had been hit.

Dave was now standing in the doorway with his forearm covering his eyes. The night sun from the helicopter circling above the barn was still switched on, searching for the Irish.

I finished his dressing as Bash came around. Chris helped him up and out to the rescue team waiting outside, and I started to get Mr X out of his trough, which very nearly became a stone coffin. His pulse had gained a bit of strength so the drip must be doing some good. (*Still a miracle*)

The lights then outside dimmed, and I could hear Dave talking, "John, I am glad to see you. We've got a man down. Not too bad but will need a stretcher. He's unconscious from a fall." As Dave said this, Bash came out supported by Chris.

"Good job lads," John shouted. Then he instructed them to get straight aboard the Wessex.

"Scrub that. In regards to him being unconscious, John."

"He's now walking injured."

Dave gave a laugh. John complemented again telling Dave……

Dave interrupted.

"Wait John there's good news! We have your Mr X. He is lucky to be alive. Steve has stabilised him and dressed all his wounds. But he is in a mess a real fucking mess John, Steve got fluids in him with a Murthy drip."

John was clearly happy something good had now come out of this operation that had gone so fucking pear shaped at the beginning. The rain was pissing down but none of us cared. The scene now was two helicopters on the ground and one still in the air. Chris and Bash were climbing into the Wessex and eight SAS men had climbed out of the Lynx and were carrying out a perimeter check searching for the mob that had shot fuck out of the barn. Loading lights were lit on the helicopters, and all you could see were lights running around. These lights were the torches attached to the SAS weapons. As Dave continued talking, two of the soldiers came from the bushes dragging a man in full combats and wearing a balaclava. The man was shouting and swearing at the SAS.

"Fucking English pigs! Dog's scum."

John left Dave and ran over to him and smacked him on the chin. The Irish terrorist went limp, the two holding him dropped him to the floor and secured his wrists and ankles with black plastic wire ties. Then they picked him up and threw him onto the Lynx. "There are three of his lot inside the barn dead John. One stabbed, and two shot."

John came back with, "Good job. Let's get your brick out of here."

I was the last in the barn out of our brick. Chris had helped Bash out. I was just explaining to one of the other medics that came with John what I had done already to Mr X. I also told him the state of his injuries to his knees and shoulder.

Just as I handed my patient over, John patted me on the back and said, "Well done, Steve. Come on. Time to go. The rest of your lot are on the helicopter."

I just looked up at him. I don't know what was in my eyes, but he said to me, "You had to do it!"

01.37 Hours

WE FLEW BACK over the border. Back to the Mill.

BRADFORD

The Mansion

THE BRIGADIER HAD just flown back to Scotland, and Arthur and I were sitting in Dave's study. We were talking and having a drink waiting for Dave. This room was in much the same deco as the rest of the house, making it look old and authentic. One wall was totally covered in shelves filled with old books which were hand bound with leather. There was one of those library ladders which ran along the shelves on rollers. On the opposite wall was a long stone fireplace with two high backed chairs, and just behind that was Dave's fantastic desk. I'm no expert, but it was either Oak or Mahogany and big. It was about eight by four feet with a wooden and leather captain's chair. In front of the desk were two wooden sturdy chairs with cushions on the seat bits.

Arthur was looking out of one of the high backed chairs next to the fire, when the door opened and Sarah and Dave came in laughing. Actually, they did make a good couple, but they quickly realised we were there. It was funny how their behaviour totally changed, instantly becoming rather professional.

"Right, thanks Sarah. I'll pass the message on," said Dave in altered tone of voice.

"I'm off to use your range for half an hour," said Sarah and the door shut behind her.

"Pull up a seat men," Dave came out with, as he made himself comfortable behind his desk. Arthur and I moved to the chairs in front of the desk.

"Dave, do you want me to start?" said Arthur.

"Start? Start what?" was my question as I glanced at them individually.

Dave started, "Well, it's like this, Steve. I want you to work full time for me as a CPO. However, there is also another position vacant that we require an apprentice for."

"And what's that?" I said.

Arthur butted in with, "It's my apprentice."

"Doing what? I'm a builder!" I told them.

"Maybe you are now, but I want you to just sit there for two minutes and listen. You don't have to give us an answer until the morning. Steve, I must ask you and I know I can trust you if you give me your word. If you accept the job nobody must know. Also if you decline then this conversation has never taken place. Do I have your word Steve?"

He held out his hand and I leaned forward, shook it and said, "Of course."

"Steve, I'll make one apology before I start. We were just going to offer you part time work for a few months and then offer you the CPO job, then maybe later invite you onto the Evolved operations. However, you were at the briefing tonight and in this line of work we have to act very fast on circumstances out of our control. I am sure you can appreciate that.'

'Here's the deal, Steve. If you accept, the minute the bank opens tomorrow I transfer £15,000 into your account, and that is just a retainer. Every CPO job you go on you will get an hourly rate or a shift rate on average a CPO with us at the moment with their retainer are earning £40,000 min per year. Now here's the clinch, Steve. I want you to be and train as an assassin."

I laughed, more out of disbelief then humour.

"Dave's not joking, Steve," Arthur said as he got up and walked to the drinks cabinet. I looked at Dave then looked at Arthur and back at Dave and shook my head.

"I know it's a lot to take in Steve, but I saw you in Ireland. Remember? I know you can do it," Dave said as he stared straight at me.

"No! No… come on you two. This is a wind up, surly?" I told them.

"Steve, you are made for the job, plus you're not fanatical or psychopathic. You have morals, empathy and judgment. You are capable of keeping your head when there are no rules," Dave finished his speech.

Arthur was pouring himself and Dave another whiskey. He had finished pouring his and with the last drop topped up Dave's. Arthur then asked if I wanted a beer. I just stared at him blank in expression. Arthur asked me again while I kept staring.

Dave raised his voice, "*Steve!*"

I turned towards Dave. "Yes," I replied.

"Do you want a drink?" Dave asked whilst pointing toward Arthur who was holding up a bottle of Becks by the neck swinging it. "You with us Steve?"

"Yes… I'm just a bit shocked with everything, to be honest. I've not been in your world for a long, long time. I'm really not up to it. I'm a builder and a dad." Dave then came back with pulling no punches, "Steve, are you sure you're not a frustrated man… a soldier who loves his kids, and gets nothing else out of his life?"

I answered Dave with, anger really and said, "Fuck you mate! I'm happy."

Dave stood up looked straight at me, and then took the Becks from Arthur. He approached me and gave me the bottle saying, "Like I said, Steve. You've got until the morning, and if you're genuinely happy with your life, I will put a grand in your bank for old times and no hard feelings."

Dave then turned back to Arthur who handed him his drink. Arthur said nothing. He didn't move. He stood there with Dave, both of them warming near the fire chatting as if they had just offered me a taxi job.

I exited the study speaking to no one. As I pulled the door to behind me, I remembered thinking Dave was spot on with everything he had just said, but I was so unsure what was actually been offered. I stood in the hall trying unsuccessfully to make sense of what was happening.

All I knew was I hadn't been happy for a long time. (*This I could not deny not to myself anyway*) Just then I noticed the lights still on in the conservatory, a bit more buffet wouldn't hurt. Walking through the door I saw John, Tanya, and Marley all standing around the buffet table laughing. Tanya and John were also filling their plates.

"Mr. Steve, would you like some food before we fold away." Marley invited

"You won't get better Chinese food anywhere else. Than here, Steve," Tanya expressed, as she placed a Chinese roll into her mouth.

Marley then clapped her hands together and bowed towards Tanya. Chang wiped a plate and offered it to me. Tanya was so right. The buffet was really exceptional as I filled the last space on my plate with a couple of ribs.

Tanya offered me a Fortune cookie. I went to grab one, but Marley stopped me. She took the dish off of Tanya, and placed a cloth over the top of it. She then made me grab one again… blind this time. I took one and put it in my shirt pocket un-opened.

"I'm going outside for a smoke," were John's words as he placed his empty plate on the table.

Chang and Marley were just clearing up the last of the buffet when Tanya asked me what I thought of the briefing.

I told her, "I'm not sure what I made of all or any of it really. The last few days had been like a dream. To say the least, I couldn't take it all in. However, I had found the cult information very disturbing yet also intriguing."

Tanya then told me that was her main task on this operation. She had been instructed yesterday to compile a dossier on the 'Lambs of God' with the intention of after Operation take Down had been executed. She would be working with the authorities to complete the end of this cult's reign. She would be giving a briefing to several countries that had to suffer at the hands of this vile Cult.

"Harold Fletchly was a man in his 50's with no conscience or empathy towards others clearly an antisocial psychopath," Tanya went on to say. (*I believe she was rehearsing her speech on me. I didn't mind.*)

"As far as we can find out, Fletchly has had at least sixty marriages of which thirty have been to girls younger than seventeen. We have a file of reports disclosing Fletchly's sickening child abuse, and we also have one credible eye's witness account from a former bodyguard of Fletchly's. That clearly states that Fletchly beat to death at least two women and one child. Then, he sodomized them before their bodies were cold and scooped the eyes out of their sockets." Tanya took a sip of her drink. Clearly disturbed just by passing on this information.

"Why isn't he in fucking jail?" I asked Tanya.

"Well, Steve, it's not for want of trying. *Believe me*. There are hundreds of Police reports, and Court case files going back twenty years. This man or creature has never been found guilty. It doesn't help the fact that the Lambs of God has been associated with the suicidal deaths of more than three hundred people in six different countries. The cult also has fourteen lawyers in its employ. Their assets and cash, what we have been able to trace, is a fortune of sixteen million pounds sterling. We believe this is approximately 60–70% of their total worth and we are at the minute putting together a law suit to seize and freeze their assets and or bank accounts in each country. We can reintegrate at least three thousand lost souls from the terror of this cult and rehabilitate them back into society.'

'To be successful in this, the monster known as Harold Fletchly has to be taken out of the picture. We believe he has a vault full of incriminating evidence on a lot of Politicians, Judges, and other powerful people. Black mail is also an issue, but we are not sure as to what level some of our political figures are involved. So much is just starting to appear, Steve, the more we fish in the murky water and now as the water settles we are seeing people that we would of never believed capable of involvement with Fletchly."

"Operation '*Take Out*' will be the permanent removal of Fletchly, and three other cult leaders and to discover the location of the vault. Once, we have all the incriminating evidence, then operation *Take Down* can be given the go ahead accumulating in the prosecution of many cult members and who or whatever is dredged up." Tanya then took yet another sip of her wine.

"I see the Judges and Politicians will no longer be in fear of documents being made public," I added.

"Correct," Tanya said. Then continued, "In the following months after the seizure of all this evidence, it will be entertaining to watch certain public figures *retire,* so to speak," Tanya laughed. She then walked up to me stood on her toes and kissed me on the cheek. I grabbed her and gave her a hug, pulling her tight into me as it had been a long time since I had any female contact.

This however was short lived, because as I pulled Tanya closer to me, she crushed the fortune cookie in my pocket. She laughed and put her petite hand into my pocket to retrieve the cookie. She then opened up the small scroll and smiled. "Let's have a look then," I said taking if off her. I read it, "Follow your heart. Follow your destiny. Well that's …" and before I could say anything else Tanya kissed me again. This time on the lips, then off she went saying good night. Standing there, finishing my beer when John re-entered the conservatory.

"Well, Steve you appear to have fitted back in nicely."

Laughing slightly I replied, "It doesn't feel like that inside my head."

John replied quite wisely, "It never does with this type of work. That's what makes it worthwhile."

"So John, what's your role on this operation?" I questioned.

"You won't really see a lot of me, Steve. I'm the Brigadier's man. I work for him with him, and only he knows what I do."

"Fucking hell, John. That's deep." We both laughed. Chan then joined us. We continued to chat a while, then we called it a night. As I walked up the great stair case, I started to think John was right I was fitting in here.

07.50 Hours KAVANAH HOUSE SCOTLAND

IAN MCPHERSON AND the Brigadier were at the breakfast table and were working to synchronize their schedules when Annabelle and the Colonel walked in.

"Morning gentleman. We have just received this letter. Well, in fact it's more like another scroll."

Ian put his pen down stood up and leaned over

towards the Colonel saying, "Would you like me to open and read it, Sir?"

The Colonel didn't reply, but just handed the scroll in the direction of Ian. The scroll was rolled up and sealed closed with wax and also tied secure with a dark ribbon.

"How was it delivered?" asked the Brigadier.

"By motorbike courier," replied Annabelle.

Ian untied the ribbon and carefully prized off the wax. The Colonel and Annabelle sat down at the table and Diane poured them a cup of tea. Ian started to read the message. As he read the scroll, Annabelle and the Colonel gazed at each other with such solemn, distraught expressions. Ian continued to read, and it was clear the message was informing the Colonel and Annabelle that Susannah intended to evict them from the family home and withdrawing funding for on-going community projects. In one week's time all the Kavanagh assets and finances solely became Susannah's.

Ian then said, "There are a couple of lines in Latin, I believe, at the top and bottom of the scroll. I don't *do* Latin."

Annabelle said, "Let me have a look Ian." Annabelle stared at the scroll not saying a word, and then a tear rolled down her cheek. She translated the words '*ut exsisto pia futures sumo sacrificial agan*', "I am honoured to be chosen to be the sacrificial lamb". '*Ego praetor responsibilities*' *of meus, sumo positus*', "I accept the responsibilities of my chosen position." Annabelle gave back the scroll to Ian and then excused herself with eyes full of tears, but too dignified to release them in front of the Brigadier and Ian.

Charles then spoke up, "Right that gives us one week to execute operation *Take Down*."

The Brigadier didn't mention Operation Take Out. (*As this was top secret and on a need to know basis*)

"Ian, my good fellow, could you start making phone calls to your people at Scotland Yard? And get the Police and Social Services on standby. I will organise my people. We will get together again in forty-eight hours which will then give us an allowance of seventy-two hours before D-Day." Charles then poured himself another cup of tea.

Ian got up and left the table saying, "I will be back later today, Colonel. I'm going to have a word with your local constabulary." He was off tapping numbers on his mobile as he walked across the large kitchen.

"Right. Charles, is there anything I can do to help? I feel frustrated," said Simon.

"Well, actually I have two men coming here to-night, and they will be carrying out surveillance on the Cults farmhouse. I would be very grateful if you could put them up here at the house as I don't want the Cult getting wind of their arrival."

"Of course, Charles, that is a given, but I was thinking of something more hands on," the Colonel said.

"Actually, you could do the initial reconnaissance with these men since you know the area," replied Charles knowing how hopeless his friend must be feeling.

Charles then asked if they could go to Simon's study, and he would brief Simon fully in regards to the operation after he had made a phone call.

Charles stood up pushing his chair away from him with the back of his legs and at the same time was sipping the last of his third cup of tea. He put the cup on the solid oak table which was dressed like a banquet, toast, bacon baguettes, scrambled eggs, marmalade, etc. None of it had even been touched, apart from the Brigadier had had a slice toast.

Leaving the kitchen, Charles followed Simon to his Study. But before he left the room Charles said to Diana, "Thank you Diana the tea was the best I have ever had."

"That is kind of you to say Brigadier. Thank you," Diana replied, then set to on clearing away the table. She realised and understood why it was only the Brigadier that had eaten anything. In her mind laying the table was helping to maintain normality. She thought to herself that she would make egg and bacon rolls with the left over's and treat the estate workers at lunch.

09.15 Hours BRADFORD

SITTING AT HIS desk in his office, Dave was placing the rim of a large white mug to his lips when Chang knocked on the door.

"Yes!" shouted Dave.

Chang pushed open the large door and said, "Your

secure mobile, Mr Dave. It is the Brigadier calling."

Dave leaned over his desk to retrieve the phone. "Thank you, Chang."

Chang bowed slightly and backed out of the office closing the door behind him. Then remaining there, for the duration of the call as if on guard duty.

Dave looked at the screen on his phone to ensure it was in secure mode. (*This was indicated with several extra digits at the start of the number*)

"Good morning, Charles. How are things in Scotland?" inquired Dave.

"Morning David. Things, as you so eloquently put it, are happening a lot faster than we anticipated with regards to Operation *Take Down*. We have been planning this for months now and we should be able to pull that off. This Kidnapping of Susannah as actually been the catalyst we've needed to set a date for this event to go ahead. A lot of countries need to get rid of this Lucifer."

Charles told him only a week, if that and Susannah has to be in our possession. He then continued speaking, "My worry Dave, is operation *Take out.*"

"How long do we have, Charles? For *Take Out*," asked Dave.

"Six days. Actually five days. We will need twenty-four hours to get Susannah to sign everything back over to her grandparents. Otherwise the Kavanagh estate and fortune will end up in the pot with the rest of the cult's assets," replied Charles.

Dave then asked, "Has the powers given the go

ahead for the Take Out?"

Charles informed him, "Not yet, Dave. But take it as if it has. I have a meeting this afternoon with the minister. It will be sorted to today. We just have the formalities to get right you know, Dave. They will give permission, but they love to fantasize about been involved."

"I totally agree, Charles," Dave answered. Then said, "What about using the Mental Health Act to annul any contracts Susannah has signed in the last three months."

"I have got two Doctors and a Social Worker on standby. However, I really do not relish the idea of having to ask the question to Simon and Annabelle," was the Brigadiers reply.

Dave then reminded him, "You have the next 24 hours Charles or the necessary documentation will not be valid or even completed lawfully. If anything should go wrong and Harold Fletchly is left alive and in position, he will have enough grounds to have the grandparents up for inciting kidnap and false imprisonment. Not to mention, the Kavanagh's will be homeless and won't have a penny to their name. And, ultimately they would go to prison." Dave could hear the Brigadier under his breath agreeing. He continued, "Don't hesitate Charles. Because they are your friends. Remember how much the Steinberg family protested when their son joined the Jones Followers. When they actually got the son back, they realised he would never sign back the assets to a two hundred year old jewellery company. You know as well as I do, Brigadier, that the chances are we will need to sedate Susannah to get here out of the cult. The young lady will probably spend six months at least in the Retreat in France for Rehabilitation."

Dave was then promptly cut off by the Brigadier saying, "Enough, Dave. Enough. I know I will bring the subject up to my friends tonight."

Dave replied, "Okay, Charles. I won't mention the subject again." He smirked his little speech had worked.

"Right. What are we doing with the waste Charles?" questioned Dave.

"Photos, DNA, Disposal," answered the Brigadier

Dave responded, "We will have a bonfire, Charles. No trace."

"Perfect! Do you think Arthur is up to the removal?" questioned Charles.

Dave replied, "I've now got Steve on board. They will be fine, Charles. Steve is one of the best second men or backups you will ever come across. I've seen it for myself."

"That will do for me, Dave. I'm sure you're aware that all our reputations will be on the line if this operation goes pear shaped."

Dave then noticing there was some recurrence in the conversation said to the Brigadier, "Chris and Basher will be in Scotland at 14.00 hours today. They have instructions to contact you on secure line when they are fifteen miles outside of your area."

Charles replied, "That's fine. I should be all wrapped up with the Minister by then. I've already arranged their accommodations and a briefing for later in the afternoon. I have also set the dead line for our next operation beefing in forty-eight hours. I want everything in place to be ready to go from that point at two hour notice."

Dave answered, "That will be possible rest assured we will be ready. I will need you to fax me a release document for the C4 explosive, 2kgs and have you arranged for the helicopters and our safe documents?"

Charles said, "I will fax it now, and Tanya has the information on the helicopters, two Wessex. I have the safe documents in my brief case to be signed by the Minister at the meeting,"

Dave replied, "Thank you, Charles. I will see you at the briefing in two days." They both put their phones down.

(Safe documents are documents that are given to the operatives that carry out operations that break the law on behalf of Governments of the said country. The documents would be in the form of a cover letter, with the contact details of a specific solicitor and MI5 administrator. Also several very official looking documents which would in a certain way explain, that what people would believe was a crime actually was a commissioned black opp. It contains the names of relevant present day high ranking politicians plus signatures and High Court Judges. Then a royal pardon is given. All this would be stamped – government stamp and Royal stamp.)

12.50 Hours M8 MOTORWAY – SCOTLAND – 24 miles outside Edinburgh.

THE WINDSCREEN WIPERS were working to full capacity, yet the view out of the van windscreen still appeared to be sub-nautical. Scotland is famous for its bad weather. On this occasion, it was truly living up to its reputation. The silver escort van at times began to actually Aqua-plane. This was giving Basher a buzz. However, Chris kept telling him to slow down.

Chris had his phone out and was working out the arrival time for Kavanagh House.

"Pull over into the next lay-by Bash," said Chris changing screens on his phone.

"Will do," Basher replied.

BANG, CRACK… were the noises heard as the van pulled sharp to the right.

"What the fuck?" shouted Chris.

Before they knew it, the van was across the all lanes of the motorway and came to a violent stop as it crashed into a post. The vehicle was now half on the verge and half on the road. Basher was still conscious; Chris though, was slumped in his seat with a one inch deep cut above his right eye. His nose and lips were bleeding and his blood was smeared all over the side window and dash.

"Chris! Chris," loudly said Basher, at the same time as pushing Chris's shoulder trying to get some reaction. No response. Basher then noticed through the cascade of water which was streaming down the windscreen oncoming lights.

Then the driver's door was flung open by a woman and a man.

"Get out!" shouted the woman and the man was now man handling Basher and pulling him out. The woman joined in the pulling. All three of them flew backwards and landed in a shallow ditch.

They then heard the sound of a loud air horn simultaneously. The silver escort with Chris still inside, spun three hundred and sixty degrees and went backwards into the ditch six feet passed Basher and his two rescuers.

The articulated lorry that had just clipped the van was screeching to a halt. Wheels locked and thick black smoke came from the burning rubber, which gave off that unmistakable nose clogging stench. The wet tarmac road and heavy rain turned the smoke into a dark grey cloud.

Basher was now at the passenger side of the van and trying to get Chris out who was now bleeding heavily from the shoulder and eye. The woman was on her mobile talking to the emergency services. She had dialled 999 and asked for the ambulance and Police. Then had been connected to an ambulance operator who was asking here lots of questions, as well as trying to inform her that the helmed 191(rescue helicopter) had been dispatched.

Even though her mobile was still physically touching her ear, she heard nothing. The man and the lorry driver had gone to help Bash get Chris out. They were all carrying him to the flat verge away from the motor way.

The Police were now on the scene and had closed off the inside lane with their Volvo estate cars and dozens of traffic cones, yellow with blue and white shiny jackets branded, '*POLICE*'.

The rain had not eased at all. The woman had run back to the lay-by where she had a takeaway cafe trailer. She grabbed all her bin liners and ran back nearly falling on the muddy grass verge as she reached Chris. She pushed Bash slightly out the way to cover his friend. Keeping the rain off. Basher still bending down next to Chris never said a word.

The blood had mixed with the running water. The scene looked horrific, resembling an 18th century slaughter house been washed out. Basher had dressed Chris's shoulder and began applying pressure now on the wound. A crowd of about fifteen people had all gathered around Chris and Basher, including two Police officers asking Bash questions.

The noise was just a blur to Bash, who at that moment felt as if he was laying on the verge. Just then, you could hear the beautiful unmistaken sound of helmed 191. Bash looked up and through scared eyes. He saw the bright yellow Sea King breaking through the clouds coming into land in the field on the other side of the motorway.

"Chris, not long now... you're off to hospital. Stay with us. Come on, Chris!" Said Bash still applying pressure to his mates wound.

Sixty Miles away in the Forrester's lodge Harold Fletchly answered his private telephone, "*Speak.*"

A Russian accent replied, "The flag has been taken down."

Then Fletchly replied, "Your compensation will be made the full amount as agreed."

The Russian then spoke a few words in his native tongue and this ended the conversation.

Motorway

"LET US THROUGH! Out of the way! Mind your backs! Coming through. We need to see the casualty," said the Paramedic assertively pushing herself physically past the now growing crowd.

Then kneeling next to Bash, "What do we have here then?" asked the female Paramedic.

"He's been unconscious for approximately twenty minutes. Deep cut to the left shoulder, which I've dressed. He's got a pulse, but weak. His name is Chris."

"Hi, Chris. I'm Debbie. Part of the air ambulance crew. We are going to put a drip into you then get you to Edinburgh Hospital."

The other medic who was still making his way to were Chris lay, asked the Police to clear the crowd away as they would need to move the casualty.

Then as he got to his mate, he knelt down and slid

a plastic bright red stretcher alongside Chris. Bash was now speaking on the mobile with Dave.

"I heard that Bash. I'll have a break down truck with you in sixty minutes. Are you able to stay with the van and the equipment?" spoke Dave.

Bash replied, "Yes, will do. I have to go we are carrying Chris over to the helicopter."

Dave said, "I'll chase up the hospital and keep you up dated Basher," and he put the phone down.

The Police had now closed off both sides of the motorway all six lanes, and Bash, two medics, and the lorry driver ran across the road with Chris strapped tightly to the stretcher. They slid the stretcher into the Sea King.

The Medics jumped on and strapped down the stretcher, swapped the fluids bag and said to Basher, "Are you coming with him?"

"No. I'll follow later," Basher said as he started to walk away from the helicopter with the lorry driver.

The Sea King lifted off and Bash grabbed the driver and pulled him down.

"We'll have to wait until it's gone, it may blow us over." The lorry driver just nodded, not really hearing Bash he had to lip read because of the noise.

Back on the other side of the six lanes, Police were taping off the escort van. The woman walked up to Bash and the lorry driver. The outside lane was now open again. The torrential rain had eased to a fine drizzle, and the sun was now visible ironically showing off a rainbow.

The traffic Police pulled their Volvo up behind the lorry. One of the officers walked over to the driver and asked him to join them in their car. The driver following the two officers shivered a couple of times as he was soaked through to the skin. The officer noticed this and opened the Volvo's hatch back and removed a silver foil blanket and gave it to the driver.

"Thank you," the driver replied as he rapped himself.

Bash looked at the van and all the blood and told himself to *pull it together.* He knew Chris would be fine now. He blinked his eyes slowly and filled his lungs with fresh air, then held on to it for a few seconds. Repeating this a couple of times helped to calm him, allowing him to become rational. (*If that was possible for Bash*) Megan, the woman's name, had asked Bash to come to her takeaway trailer and have a cup of tea.

Bashers pocket started to vibrate again. He grabbed his phone and as he pressed the receive button. At the same time, he told Megan he was going to stay with the van. Little did Megan know that there was about £15,000 of top military equipment and an M107.50 Calibre Sniper Rifle and a M14 US Infrared night scope. As you can imagine the Police would have a few questions.

Bash answered his phone "Hello?"

"Hi, Tony. This is Ian McPherson. I work with the Brigadier. I'm an inspector at Scotland Yard, so if any of the Police try and open the van tell them no. Give them my name and rank. I will text you a telephone number they can ring if they get clever. I'm on my way to meet with you, I hope Chris will be ok."

"Thanks, Ian. I will see you when you get here."

Bash who was leaning on the van, with both elbows on the roof and his chest resting against the door switched off his phone. He looked up to see Megan slipping her way across the wet, muddy verge with a cup of something steaming hot and a sandwich.

Bash smiled and said as she neared. "Thanks, Megan." Pushing himself of the van by preforming a standing press up. He accepted the drink, and then took a gulp of the tea. He leaned fully back on the van and reflected on what had just happened to put his closest friend in hospital.

Megan aware of the trance like state he was in, left him to himself. She placed the sandwich on top of the van next to where his cup was, and then walked back to her trailer bar. He had just finished the last drop of tea, when the Police car doors opened and the officers and the lorry driver got out. The driver walked towards his lorry and the two policemen headed in Basher's direction as the officers got up to Bash.

Basher's first words were, "You can't blame the driver. He didn't have a chance of stopping."

The tall Police Officer asked Basher, "Are you injured?"

"I'm bruised, but that's it," replied Bash.

The second stocky shorter officer was now looking around the van whilst his colleague spoke with Bash.

"Can you tell us what you think happened?" was

the next question asked as the Constable started writing in his note book. Before Bash replied the stocky copper beckoned his partner to come and look at something.

"What do you make of this?"

The tall officer walked round to the side of the escort van where his colleague was squatting down next to the near side front wheel. The stocky officer had his finger in a hole in the tire.

"Gunshot," said the tall officer.

His colleague just nodded with an expression of agreement. Bash had followed the officer around and when he saw the bullet hole said,

"That must have been a powerful rifle to do that at the speed we were going."

"Do you know about weapons," asked the short stocky copper who had now stood up.

"I was in the army for a few years," replied Bash. Then the questions started.

"Do you have any idea why someone would want to shoot at you?"

"Where are you heading?"

"Can we have a look in the van?"

Basher told the officers, "Chris and I were just going camping and fishing for a week. I have no idea why someone shot at us, and no. I would prefer you not to look in the van."

The two Officers started to talk to each other quietly. Then they walked up to Basher and asked for the vehicle's keys. Just then, Basher's phone received a SMS text message, Bash quickly opened the message.

"Before you approach the van read this," and he passed the phone over to the tall officer. The message stated:

> **13.26,06/09/2001 SMS received 0798959164 Inspector I. McPherson – 64621 – Scotland Yard. The vehicle registration reg: TR50 LEW – Silver Escort Van is not to be entered or tampered with at any cost by any persons. Please cordon off this vehicle until the arrival of myself (call 0233532000) Whitehall ext 241.**

The tall officer turned and walked away a few paces and with his right hand pressed his radio and asked to speak to the duty inspector. He asked if the inspector could call him back on his mobile…

"Just secure the vehicle for now until the inspector calls back," said the tall officer to his colleague.

Ian McPherson had just set off from Kavanagh House. He had contacted the local Police who also set off followed by a Police Tow Truck. They were all now on route to meet with Bash.

BRADFORD

DAVE SWIVELLED AROUND on his chair and grabbed the fax coming out of his machine. He opened a file on his desk and removed several papers and then stapled the authorisation fax to them and placed it all in an envelope. Then throwing the envelope in his brief case. Dave left his office and Marley was waiting for him in the hall with his jacket and pack up box.

Dave smiled when he took the pack up from Marley. The large external door was then opened by Chang.

"Have a good day, sir."

"And you, Chang. Tell Marley we won't need any tea making this evening."

Chang did his small half respectful bow, "Thank you, Mr Dave." And he closed the door.

The Range Rover pulled up at the bottom of the stone stairs, and Dave got into the passenger side. All you then heard was the sound of rubber crushing gravel as the vehicle shot off away from the house.

M62 EAST BOUND

I HAD JUST passed the Humber Bridge. I was about seven miles from Hull when the new mobile phone that Dave had given me earlier started ringing.

It was the standard Nokia tune and the phone was one of them Nokia N95's I think.

"Hello?" I said sliding the phone up.

"Good afternoon, Steve," replied Tanya.

Well, the second I heard her voice it was like a Doctor injecting a patient's dead heart with adrenalin and it started beating again. She brought me to life.

"Hi, Tanya," I attempted to say it as casually as I could.

"Steve, I have been asked to ring you as there has been an accident in Scotland involving…."

I cut Tanya short, saying, "Not Chris and Bash?"

"Yes, I'm afraid so, and I'm sorry to be the bearer of bad news. Bash is okay, however Chris has been air lifted to Edinburgh Hospital. He is in surgery now."

Tanya took a breath, then continued, "Dave has been on the phone with the hospital and Chris will be okay. He has a very deep wound to his shoulder and sustained some internal bleeding" Tanya stopped again.

"Good as long as they are alive," I spoke.

Tanya was sitting at her desk whilst on the phone to me. Her desk was very modern stainless steel legs and solid one piece glass top. With four monitors and a large stack of computers in like a wire cage stand next to the desk. All the monitors were on, and they were all different from the next. The first screen had just account details as did the second. However the third screen was showing a man carrying out an inspection on a Wessex helicopter. The fourth had just a screen saver on it, which were the words '*Top Secret*'. These words floating around the screen.

Sitting against this monitor was an old hand made tatty rag doll with one eye missing and the other was a red button the doll had clearly seen much better days. (*It had been loved*) Tanya's office was in a very well to do area of Kensington. It was an apartment which had been converted in to three offices and a meeting room. The remaining two offices were occupied by well you could say two more Tanya's. They were also PA's to high ranking officers who were in charge of clandestine departments. The three offices were in like a horse shoe shape and all of the fronts were glass and facing into a reception area. However at the flick of a switch, the front of each office the all farced would turn blue instantly privatising the individual office.

The reception area was not modern in design and leaned to the old fashioned. There were two antique brown leather chairs and a large day sofa. In the left corner of the room, there was an 18th century drinks cabinet which was playing host to several spirits and a couple of bottles of tonic water. Covering the walls was 18th century wooden panelling which complemented the room's ornaments and matching architectural features. The whole room really could have been pinched from a Conan Doyle Sherlock Holmes movie.

Tanya was a twenty-seven year old, very well spoken, well-educated young lady. You could have been forgiven for surmising that she had come from an upper class family. When in fact, she had started life in a Chinese orphanage (*not named*). Tanya's life as far as anyone knows is only documented from her 2nd birthday.

When she was six years old, an English couple adopted her. The couple were living in China as part of their jobs. As Tanya's new father was a trade minister for England. The couple were about to return to England after serving four's years in China, so they decided to take a month off to travel around rural China and see this lovely country before they left.

Into their second week travelling, they visited an orphanage. They got to talking to an elderly gentleman who was a British Citizen. He was also a missionary who had spent the last 25 years in China. As well as running his mission he was helping with education and supporting the local orphanage with donations and medical assistance. Due to the Chinese rule of only having one child per family, orphanages would end up taking in a lot of thrown away babies usually girls as the Chinese put a preference on the male lineage.

Now according to the Missionary some of the orphanages would be forced to have Kull to bring down the number of children every two or three years. The children would be given a last supper containing poison and then during the night the bodies were taken by horse and cart from the orphanage for disposal by fire a few miles outside the villages.

Tanya, known to then as Tia, was just turning six years old and because she was of mixed race. In fact, even then, according to reports, was more European than Asian. She would be on the next Kull list for certain. Jeremy, the missionary who had been educating Tia, was determined that this would not happen. Sarah and Jonathan, Tanya's future parents, basically purchased Tia and got a promise from the orphanage that the Kull which was due to take place in a week's time would be cancelled.

This cost £5000, however very happy they had saved not only Tia but at least twenty children Sarah and Jonathan had clinched the deal which made them happy now presented the new instant parents with the problem of getting Tia or Tanya out of China and home with them without any paper work. Luckily for Jonathan, his brother, Charles, was a major in the British Army carrying out special operations. Jonathan contacted Charles.

After a lengthy conversation on the telephone between Charles and Jonathan a plan had emerged. Sarah and Jonathan would continue with their sightseeing holiday taking Tia with them. It would take them at least twelve to fourteen days to cover the vast distance from Hohhot to the Tibetan border where they had a rendezvous with Charles. He would then smuggle Tia/Tanya through Tibet and into Nepal. Waiting for them there with family paperwork and all the documentation would be a middle aged couple called Chang and Marley.

Tia on paper would now be part of their family their daughter and they all had permits to enter the UK for a 28 day stay to visit relatives. It took Charles seven days to get Tanya through Tibet to Korari where she was handed over to Marley and Chang.

The moment Marley saw Tia she cupped her hands around the child's little face and said, "You are so beautiful and very blessed."

Tia smiled and softly spoke, "Toe chic." The six year old little girl who had just spent a rough seven days crossing Tibet, conquering the challenging terrain with an SAS soldier was in very good spirits. Charles had carried Tia like a ruck sack half the distance, but Tia had also ran and slept like a soldier... not once complaining.

Her clothes were nothing but rags. Luckily, Marley brought with her a bag full of traditional western clothes for Tia, and also a small rag woollen doll with red buttons for eyes. Marley, then took Tia by the hand and led her down to the edge of the river stripped her clothes off and washed her.

Meanwhile, up the bank, Chang had poured Charles a cup of tea from a flask. He then gave Charles the documents to look at – visa's, travel permits and passports. All these included Tia as a family member Daughter.

Just then, Tia and Marley returned from the river. Tia now clean and dressed in fresh clean clothes looked like a different girl. Charles then gave the paperwork back to Chang and said farewell. Charles walked approximately forty feet from the others when Tia's name was shouted by Marley. Which alerted Charles, who turned around. Tia ran straight up to him and threw her arms around his thighs, squeezing as tight as the little petite creature could.

Charles knelt down and grabbed her by the shoulders and looking her straight in the eyes said, "I will see you in England in one weeks' time."

Tia could not yet speak a lot of English, but thanks to Jeremy the Missionary she managed a bit and understood some. Tia nodded her little head and smiled. Charles kissed her forehead and then stood up. By then, Chang and Marley had got up to them Marley put her arm around Tia.

The day, from that moment on, seemed to brighten. Charles walked away with a place now occupied by Tanya in his heart. One that would never become vacant.

Charles was in his middle thirties, single and had no children of his own with only one sibling. His mother had tragically died from Malaria when he was a small child of only seven. She'd caught this awful disease whilst on a diplomatic posting in the Netherlands has Charles's father was a foreign diplomat. His farther had done his best for the boy's and this included them going to residential boarding school from the age of nine until they turned eighteen. On the outside Charles's persona was distant and emotionless learning at a very early age not to get attached.

His brother was very different. He had suffered a lot of illness as a child and spent time growing up with his grandmother been nursed. He then left school and went to university then after getting two degrees, following his father and grandfather into the diplomatic core.

Charles was so different to his older brother. He clearly came from his mother's side of the family which was historically military and revolved around honour, structure and the establishment. An old, family I believe is what they call them.

He was a powerful and very fit man who had the respect of a lot of soldiers and officers alike. He was also a high ranking officer with the SAS but he had not been given the rank. Charles clearly deserved it as he had completed and passed the SAS selection which is the toughest in the world.

Charles had once been in love with and courted a girl for eighteen months. He had known this girl most of his life on and off. She was a family friend, but at the age of twenty-five, he broke the engagement of with his sweet heart. He then committed himself totally to his career. Annabelle was heartbroken, as she truly loved Charles. Stupidly he believed he was doing the best for Annabelle!

Scotland M8

IAN MCPHERSON, ALONG with the Police breakdown truck, had just reached Bash. The inside lane of the M8 motorway was still closed and the Police had totally taped and cordoned off the van. Bash was sitting in a red striped folding deck chair loaned to him by the lorry driver. He had perched himself right up as close as he could to the escort.

Walking up close to Bash, Ian put out his hand and introduced himself, "Hi, Tony. I'm Ian. I spoke on the phone with you earlier."

Bash wobbling the flimsy chair as he pushed himself up, shook Ian's hand. "Hi Ian. So you work alongside the Brigadier?"

Ian then gestured to Bash to sit back down at the same time saying, "Just before we arrived here, I got a phone call from Tanya. She informed me that Chris has just gotten out of surgery and he is stable. He is expected to do well and make a full recovery."

Then he answered Basher's question, "Yes, I am the liaison officer between the Brigadier and the Police. Whatever the Brigadier needs to do, John executes the work with him. Tanya and I make it official. Which is not always easy as I'm sure you will appreciate." He laughed

Bash also laughed and replied, "I do we call the Brigadier's department X files." They both laughed again.

Ian then looked around and coming towards them was Megan again from the snack bar with some more drinks.

"You've been well looked after here, Tony." Commented Ian.

"Yes, Ian," replied Bash as Megan handed him yet another drink.

"Where is the lorry driver gone?" Megan asked Bash.

"The Police have taken him to hospital as he came over all faint and felt nauseous," replied Bash.

"Does that mean that drinks going spare," inquired Ian.

"Yes, its tea and one sugar." Megan handed it to him.

Ian then asked, "How much?"

"Nothing, don't be silly," was Megan's reply shaking her hand left to right with the palm downwards. Then Megan was gone again.

Ian took a sip of his tea then said, "Tony we have a hire van on the back of the Tow Truck. When you're ready, we will swap the equipment over from the escort to the hire van. How do you feel regards driving?"

"Call me Bash, Ian. I can drive. I'm ok now I

know Chris is going to pull through." Bash must have taken a shine to Ian as he told him to call him Bash.

You could hear the sentiment when he talked about Chris, and I can vouch for this close relationship they had from when I was in the Army with them. They just gelled. (*Imagine Ant and Deck but taller and more muscular*)

The time now was 16.14 hours. The Police at the scene had been over and spoke with Ian. After seeing his warrant card, they were happy for him to take over. The police tow truck pulled away with the silver escort on its back, followed by Ian. Bash reversed up to Megan's take away trailer but only to find the shutters had been closed. There was no sign of the sandwich angel. He was slightly saddened that he would not be able to say thanks to this kind lady, but Bash was ready to shoot off.

Then just as he was winding up his window, Megan appeared from behind the snack bar smiling and saying, "So you were going to leave without saying good bye." Megan smiled.

Bash reversed the direction his hand was winding and the window went down wards again.

Bash then rolled is bum cheek of the car seat and removed his wallet and grabbed a twenty pound note out of it, he offered this to Megan and said, "Please except this for all the food and drinks." Bash extended his arm out of the van window gesturing Megan to take the money.

Megan's smile dispersed and a slightly insulted look

appeared. She knew Bash was been nice and didn't mean any disrespect, but she had helped for the sake of helping not for financial gain.

Megan was stood there next to the van window in the rain wearing chef's whites and now on top of these had been thrown on a flimsy tatty purple jacket. The bottoms of the white trousers were caked in mud from all of the angel's trips back and forth from the take away to the accident scene.

If the truth be known, that twenty pounds Bash was offering would have helped Megan a lot. She was the owner of the snack bar from which she made a living for herself and her four year old downs syndrome son, Alfie. Megan was a thirty-five year old down to earth, nice person, yet life had not treat her well. She looked over forty and she was not wearing any makeup. Her hair was a mess, resembling a wench from the eighteen hundreds.

She had been single for about three years after escaping from an abusive relationship. The last act of violence dished out to her was when she was fleeing the family home. She had reached the bottom of four flights of stairs in this block of maisonettes on the Dumbiedykes' council estate in Edinburgh, when her partner threw a television set down on her. It only just missed as she stood there cradling Alfie.

Megan did not want to take the money and she told Bash, "Put it back in your wallet."

"Please take it," Bash replied.

But then for the first time in years, (*Bash told me*

later) he looked into Megan's eyes and saw all the sadness and worry, yet he could still see the love and kindness she had to offer. (Bash had a moment)

"If you want to thank me for today, take me out with that money," Megan told him. Then she quickly back tracked by saying, "Stupid me. Why would someone like you take me out?"

Then there was just silence. Bash being Bash didn't have a clue what to say, so he got back in the van and drove off. But then he stopped twenty or so feet from Megan. He got out of the van and walked back to her. He gave her the twenty pounds, placing it in her hand then curled up her fingers.

"You keep that and I will take you out as well," he told her with a smile.

Megan kept old of the money and kissed Bash. Then her cheeks went bright red. Bash removed his wallet again this time removing a business card, with the words 'Security Consultant' printed on it along with his name and number underneath.

"Call me if you want," Bash told her.

Megan kissed him again and said nothing.

———————

By 16.35 hours, Bash was back on the road heading towards Kavanagh house. At the exact same time, I was getting out of my shower at home. Arthur was picking me up at 18.10 hours and we were going to Humberside Airport.

We were flying from there at 20.20 hours and due to land at Edinburgh at 21.10 hours. Tanya had chartered us a private plane. We were originally driving up to Scotland, however, since the crash, Dave had rang Arthur. He informed him that it looked like the Cult knew we are onto them. It was confirmed by Ian McPherson that the van tire was shot out with a very powerful weapon. It must have been from a considerable distance which would have taken the skills of a trained professional sniper.

Arthur was ranting, "How do they know? How could they have found out?"

Dave's reply was simple, "Arthur, we may have underestimated this. Harold Fletchly and the reach he has is more than we anticipated." Dave sounded unusually quiet and there was caution in his tone.

"But still, Dave. There are only a handful of us that know what's going on!" ranted again Arthur.

"Arthur, that's only this little bit that we are dealing with. Don't forget that operation *Take Down* has around eighty people involved."

"Yes, Dave. I agree with that, but they would not have all known about the van going to Scotland. That's my point," spitted out Arthur.

"For fuck sake mate! Don't you think I know that," snarled Dave. But then he quickly apologised with, "Sorry, Arthur. It's just getting to me. I cannot work out how they found out about the van, and it sticks in my throat to think one of our team as squealed." Dave was hurt.

Arthur came back with, "Well, who actually knows Dave?"

Dave started saying names, "Chris, Bash, you, me, Tanya, the Brigadier, Chang, Darren, Pete and Sarah. There are a couple more that know we are doing something up in Scotland but not about the van. If a sniper took the wheel out, that means planning and time," Dave finished.

"They must have somehow gotten us under surveillance, Dave," Arthur replied as he crossed off every name Dave just mentioned.

Arthur was scribbling the names on a piece of paper. He had written them down for the second time, when he started to draw a time line plan. He started with the van crashing then one line to the left. Then he dropped down and made eleven small branches, one for each name Dave had mentioned.

Arthur finished drawing, then said Dave, "Leave this with me. I'll work on this and get back to you."

"Thanks, Arthur. I'm going to have to get going to meet the Brigadier. We are going to be discussing the same subject. Because if we don't find the leak, we can't continue. Someone would get killed." Receiver down.

Arthur had crossed off eight of the names leaving three branches, Sarah, the Brigadier and Pete. Arthur had drunk another three cups of coffee and had managed to eliminate both Sarah and Pete from his incident tree. The Brigadier's name, however had started with one little branch on the time line and had grown into its own entirety.

After an hour or so the Brigadier's name had led to Ian McPherson. Ian was one of the first to be involved in this investigation and although not personally involved with our side. Arthur had seduced that if any tails or surveillance could have been attached to us the realistic possibility was Ian and the local police station.

Arthur speed dialled Tanya on his mobile…

"Hi, Arthur," Tanya answered with.

"Has any information been sent to Ian McPherson regards us specifically the escort van?"

Tanya told him, "Yes"

Arthur replied, "What and when was the contact made?"

"One second." There was a small silence before Tanya continued, "Here it is. He requested details of the transport and approximate times. He asked for this in case he was contacted by any local Police, so he could control any possible incidents? He asked for this to be sent by secure fax to an unknown police station." Tanya then hesitated.

"What's wrong?" questioned Arthur.

"Ian requested this information from Sue two days ago. She faxed it, but made a note saying that Ian said don't worry anyone about this. Nothing will probably go wrong," Tanya finished reading.

"Where's Sue at now? Contact her and let's find out exactly what was sent," Arthur demanded.

Tanya replied, "That's just it Arthur. Sue was involved in a hit and run last night. She is critical in the hospital."

Arthur told her, "Dave is in a meeting right now with the Brigadier. Get in contact with them both, and let them know what we have found out."

Arthur switched off his phone and started to speed dial Bash. At the same time, he grabbed his bag and car keys and left his house. Now, in his car with still no answer from Bash, so he called me.

"You on your way?" I answered with.

"Yes." He replied

"Listen Stephen, no time to explain. Have you got Bash's phone number?"

"No."

Arthur said, "I'll forward it to you. Keep trying to get hold of him, and if you talk to him, tell him to get the van to a public car park. Get him to a safe place. Don't leave a message Steve."

"Fuck me, Arthur. What's going on?"

"All I will say is… Tits up. Shit has hit the fan. Big style. However, you want to word it, be with you in a bit" Arthur's phone went dead.

My phone beeped with a message. I opened the text message, saved Bash's number and started ringing.

21.00 Hours

OUR PLANE WAS circling in a queue 2000 feet above Edinburgh airport waiting for space and clearance to land. Arthur's phone received a text which read…

Range Rover Vorge reg ……….. tools in usual place – call when you're mobile.

The message was from Tanya. I had now been brought up to speed during the plane journey. We had also been bombarding Bash's phone with texts saying:

Bash, Chris had taken a turn for the worse. Please call Dave.

We landed and disembarked. When we exited the airport, there was a man stood with a card held up with *Arthur* written on it. We approached the man who looked like Phil Mitchell on steroids. He handed me a set of vehicle keys, and then pointed to a black range rover in the car park. We walked to the Range Rover and the walking muscle got into an audio.

We left the airport and had been driving for at least fifteen minutes when Arthur pulled over into a lay-by and parked. He got out of the car and went to the back of the vehicle. After, he opened the back/ boot door, he asked me to join him. I stood there with Arthur at the back of the beautiful Range Rover.

Arthur suddenly said, "This is the start Steve operation *Take Out*." Arthur then lifted up the parcel shelf and taped on the bottom of the shelf were two pistols a 9 mm browning and a colt.

"Here you go, Steve." Arthur ripped of the black duct tape and handed me the Browning along with a zipped plastic grey envelope that contained four clips of ammunition. (*Thirteen rounds in each*)

The first thing I did was press the rounds (*bullets*) in the clips/magazines. As anyone who uses weapons knows to never completely fill the magazine as this over works the spring in the mag. This can cause stoppage, costing you your life. I removed a round out of each mag as did Arthur.

I was standing there in a lay-by in the dark with a browning in my right hand and feeling no nerves. Nothing. It felt natural. It was like been back home after a long trip away. I knew that from literally this moment onwards, *this was my life*. There is this feeling you have when you were doing an operation or even an exercise. You were actually putting your life in danger, but strangely, you feel removed from mundane reality. Your world became faster. You were on the edge. This was real, and it somehow mattered what you did. I guess this was the same reason people play these computer games. The only difference being if your character gets killed, you could not just reset the game and start again.

Arthur had a black cloth bag about eighteen inches long closed with a draw string on the top. He was about to pull open the neck of the bag when his phone rang, he handed the bag to me and answered his phone,

"Arthur speaking."

"It's me, Bash."

Just the word *Call* had displayed on Arthurs phone. "You okay, Bash?" blurted out Arthur, followed by, "Where are you?"

My ears had pricked up when I had heard Arthur say Bash. As Arthur was trying to find out where Bash was. I was nudging Arthur and weirdly and exaggerating moving my lips asking, "Is he alright?"

Arthur nodded his head to me then continued questioning again, "Where are you now?"

Bash came back with, "I'm at Edinburgh Hospital. I got all your texts, but couldn't reply on my phone. Something is wrong with it."

Arthur asked, "Where is the van?"

"In the car park. Ian McPherson is keeping an eye on it," replied Bash.

Arthur then handed over his phone to me and at the same time asked for my phone. I gave him my mobile as I asked Bash how Chris was doing.

"He's fine. Still sedated, but the Doc says he will be fine." Bash paused a second and then asked what was with all the texts and phone calls.

"Not fully sure at the moment, mate."

By now Arthur had closed the back of the vehicle. He got back in the driver's seat of the Range Rover, but left the door open. I walked towards where he was sitting. He gestured to me with his hand to give him his phone back and I complied.

"Basher, its Arthur again. I have Dave on the other phone. I'm going to put you both together and Dave will give you some more information. See you in a bit Bash."

Arthur locked mobiles together with the black duct tape. He gave them to me to hold and said, "Get in, Steve," as he slammed his door.

I went round to the passenger side, lifted up the mobiles and they were now dead. I got in the vehicle and gave Arthur his phone. He placed it back in his pocket then put his foot down on the accelerator and we were gone.

"We're off to the hospital to meet Bash. Dave has briefed him and told him to stay in the hospital with Chris until we get there. I hope I'm fucking wrong Steve about Ian," Arthur mumbled aloud and then we were doing 80 mph following the satellite navigation.

23.44 hours

THE CHEQUERED FLAG appeared on the satellite navigation just as we turned out of an ugly industrial street to see the old Victorian building named Edinburgh Royal Hospital. Due to the poor street lighting and Scottish drizzle, we slowly hunted an empty parking space.

In the presence of Evil.

SIXTY-FOUR MILES IN another direction, outside Stirling in a 17th Century Manor House. The house was advertised to the outside world as a residential home called Forester's Lodge. Harold Fletchly sat on an original Jacobean arm chair, throne like in style. Its tapestry upholstered back, arms and seat which was fixed to the 16th century carved oak frame with a gold leaf covering. The room itself had dimensions of thirty-five feet in length and twenty feet in width with ten feet in height to the ceiling. In the centre of the far wall was a magnificent fire place.

The opening of the fire was five foot square, and in its centre was a three foot oblong wrought iron dog crate. The surrounding frame was black and green marble with two round pillows carved from the same stone. It had Romanesque golden pad stones on the top of them supporting the ridiculously large but artistically beautifully carved stone mantel piece.

The walls were covered with large portrait pictures six feet wide and seven feet tall hung in exquisite carved frames again, gold leaf or painted. The ceiling was segmented by massive plaster squares and rectangles individually decorated. Most of the rooms remaining furniture would have looked at home in Paris the Louvre, apart from one chair and a desk in simple form.

These two pieces were from the same era as all the ornate furniture, but were just very basic plain. These were against the left rear wall as you entered the grand room, next to an ancient wooden door with ridiculously oversized wrote iron hinges and lock. On the plain desk was a half melted candle standing in black stick holder and laying on the desk next to this were a couple of quills.

On opening, the lid of this scribes desk you found a large ornate key and antique leather bound book with a padlock/ clasp around it. When the old wooden door opened, it was as if you could hear tubular bells playing. (*The sounds of entering hell*)

Fletchly was a fifty-six year old man. He was five feet eight inches tall, an overweight man with piercing grey/ blue eyes. The story behind the resurrection of this beast started in the US in 1984 as Tanya informed me. I will tell you exactly the same as she told me pulling no punches. I will continue to call him Fletchly as not to get confused with his other alias.

Fletchly was in his last year as a medical student in an Ilano Hospital, and in the final months of his training. There had been several unexpected deaths on his ward. The hospital administration was determined to avoid a scandal related to these deaths, so instead of informing the police and coroner, they covered up the mess. Then, they forced Fletchly to take another post covering several residential homes for the elderly in Denver Colorado.

By not prosecuting Fletchly and allowing him to get away with murder enable the birth of this godless demon. Fletchly soon realised that, as well as killing for pleasure, he was able to manipulate his vulnerable patients into giving him gifts. Some even left thousands of dollars in their Will to this beast as they took their last breath.

After approximately twelve months and four assisted deaths, Fletchly had a wealth of $175,000 dollars. He used this fortune to purchase his own residential home called Angels Place. This was a thirty-six bed building similar to a hospital on one story lot. It was surrounded by lovely well maintained gardens. Supplied outside were about eight or nine electric scooters, and charger points for free use by the residents. There was also a fish pond and a small golf course present on the grounds.

There was a communal entertainments' hall and a multitude of therapy rooms for the residents to choose from. After successfully getting the banks help to finance the purchase of Angels' place, the clients would still pay $900 a month for all of these amenities.

Fletchly was raking in the cash and for once was doing nothing wrong, apart from squandering all the profits from the home. He used the money for flash cars, girls, prostitutes, drugs and gambling. He really just left the staff to run the place as he was enjoying a playboy/ Hollywood lifestyle.

Jean was the senior carer nurse at Angels Place. She was coming up to retirement age but had been in nursing all of her life. She had worked hard at the home for the last seventeen years. Jean was around five foot three inches tall and of a slender curvy build. She was not a woman to be messed with as Harold Fletchly would discover.

Angels Place was visited one Tuesday morning by the bank manager that had supported and mortgaged the home. The bank had concerns that for the last seven months Fletchly had been spending more money then what was coming in. He had also taken out $150,000 dollar loan for an extension creating another sixteen bedrooms. Fletchly had spent this money on a fifty foot yacht instead. Mr Jameson the bank manager remained at the home for nearly seven hours. He insisted that he viewed all the accounts and over looked the expenditure sheets as well as interviewing key personnel of which Jean was one of.

Mr Jameson had known Jean for twelve years since she was the main financial controller for the day to day expenses of the home. She also counter-signed on the accounts of residents who had no family or next of kin. Hours after the bank manager had left the home basically informing Fletchly, that he had a one month to stop the lavish spending and repay the $150,000 building extension loan. If the manager was not satisfied, he told Fletchly that he would inform the Police and the home inspectors.

Harold summoned Jean to his office and Fletchly was not happy. Jean had told the bank manager of all the cash that had been put down to expenses for running the home, when in fact Fletchly was signing at least $1000 – $1500 dollars a week for himself.

Jean knocked on Fletchly's office door and then entered. Fletchly was pacing back and forth behind his desk like a caged big cat waiting to be fed.

"*CLOSE THE DOOR*!!" Fletchly bawled at Jean.

Jean obeyed and closed the door then turned around to face the desk again.

"Hey!" screamed Jean as she was forced to jump backwards as Fletchly had escaped from behind his desk and had come to feed upon her.

Fletchly started shouting at Jean, "What are you fucking playing at? You evil cow."

Jean replied, "I won't stand by and watch you ruin our home."

Fletchly was surprised and silenced momentarily by the assertive direct response from such a small statured person. Fletchly who was not used to been spoken back to like that however he also was not daft and he knew Jean was a key and well respected member of the home and its surrounding community.

"Get the fuck out," then blurted Fletchly.

Jean backed to the door only turning at the last moment to twist the handle and get out quick. Slamming the door behind her Jean kept hold of the round door knob for a few moments whilst she got her bearings. She was forced to take a couple of deep breaths from the fear she had just faced. Whilst she was standing there, she could hear Fletchly on the other side of the door smashing up his cage and growling.

Jean had been frightened and yet stood her ground. This, I believe, is what saved her life and ultimately helped save some of the resident's lives and the home. That night Jean visited one of her friends on her way home. As well as being a good friend, Chief Fred Massey was in charge of the local Police force. Jean told Fred all what had been going on plus she emphasised to Fred that she had this uneasy feeling about Fletchly. Fred told Jean that he would make an official note of Jean's concerns and told her to call him day or night if she needed him.

Several weeks later and nothing had really happened. At least nothing that Jean knew about.

Fletchly had on the surface altered his ways and even apologised to Jean for his outburst and asking her for assistance in getting the home back on its feet. Jean didn't fully believe that Fletchly was sincere, but she like any good nurse played to the doctor's narcissistic traits.

Fletchly's big mistake was to under estimate Jean, and with help from her friend Chief Fred Massey, they kept an eye on this creature. Several months had passed, and Fletchly had got the bank off his case. He had now started to embezzle funds again. He was not wasting the money. This time he was creating false ID's and stashing the money.

Three deaths had occurred at the home and even though they left a lot of money, to the home itself, the deaths didn't appear suspicious.

Now another year had passed, and Jean was just starting one of her night shifts. It had just gone past eleven and Jean was in the laundry when one of her co-workers came in to help her.

"What's wrong with Mrs Western?" asked the co-worker.

"Nothing as far as I know," replied Jean.

"Dr Fletchly was giving her an injection in her bedroom as I passed a few minutes ago."

On hearing this, Jean ran to Mrs. Western's room as she arrived at her door, Fletchly was sitting on her bed indeed giving Mrs. Western an injection. He turned around, and Jean was frozen with fear. He was playing God and the sickening smile and pure delight in his eyes was terrifying. Fletchly then looked back into Mrs Weston's eyes as she died. In some sinister way, it appeared he sucked out her soul.

Jean become enraged and grabbed a fire extinguisher off the wall. She then ran, smashing the red cylinder on Fletchly's head. The extinguisher fell to the floor and exhausted white foam. Fletchly, now unconscious, fell into the foam.

Whilst Jean tried in vain to resuscitate Mrs. Western another member of staff rang for the Police and Ambulance. When the call came into the police dispatcher, Chief Massey was informed. As soon as the Angels Place was mentioned, the chief grabbed his gun belt and jacket and ran out of the door. One of deputies followed. When they arrived at the home, Fletchly had just started to re-gain consciousness and was staggering around. The chief immediately ran to Fletchly and handcuffed him. He then turned to his deputy, pushing the dazed Fletchly to him. He gave the deputy orders to take him outside to the Ambulance to be looked over. He told him that no one was to remove the handcuffs.

Fletchly was later sentenced to eighteen months custodial sentence in an open prison. He could not be prosecuted for the murder of Mrs. Weston, but was found guilty of seven counts of fraud.

The year was now 1986 and Fletchly was coming to the end of his incarceration after serving only ten months. During his ten months stay at this so called prison, Fletchly had met a twenty-nine year old man African man named Wade. Wade was a very menacing looking individual, standing at six foot seven with thick afro hair. He had flared nostrils with tribal scars on his left cheek, and his biceps were ripping his shirt.

Pastor Wade, as he was known, was imprisoned for his involvement in selling human body parts for medicine and voodoo curses. The pastor had his own church where he was the Preacher and leader of a flock of three hundred followers. As Fletchly was approaching the final months of his sentence, he had started visiting Wade at his church. On one of these occasions, he'd walked into one of the back rooms of the so called holy place. There was Wade fucking a twenty something white girl over a table. In the left corner of the semi-darkened room were two more young women huddled together. They were scantily dressed in ripped dirty rags and perched on a well-worn mattress full of bodily fluid stains.

When Wade saw Fletchly, he grabbed the female's hair lifting her head up and said to Fletchly, "Do you want to make use of this?"

Severely twisting the sex slave's head pointing her open mouth towards Fletchly. Noticing the several open cuts on the face of this girl and the fact her teeth had been removed, Fletchly said to Wade, "I see you have made her mouth cock friendly."

Wade started to laugh deeply and replied, "Ah yes, I've removed her teeth. Can't trust these bitches!" His laughter boomed again. He twisted her head further around as to entice Fletchly, then SNAP! Her neck was broken.

"Fucking hell," said Wade as he pulled out his cock. The now limp body flopped to the floor.

The other two girls were screaming so Wade took a

belt to them beating the slaves and telling them to be quiet. Fletchly walked over to the dead girl and bent down took hold. He dragged her carcass back on the table, then dropped his trousers to his ankles and started to penetrate her lifeless body. As he was opening her eye lids with his fingers, he said laughing to Wade.

"Can't waste her. She's still warm," Fletchly snickered as he ejaculated still staring into the corpse eyes.

Wade boomed with a deep sadistic laughter yet again. The other girls were still uncontrollably sobbing. They were cut and bruised from head to toe.

Over the next couple of months Wade and Fletchly had held meetings and agreed on a partnership. Some of the meetings were official involving lawyers with regards to real estate and assets that Wade already owned. Well, the church owned collectively but Wade saw it as his.

Fletchly had stashed away a small fortune of $150,000 dollars. Within the next three months, Fletchly and Wade had doubled their followers at the church and also opened a church ranch. This was the place where followers of the church could live and be a part of this new utopia. The ranch was named *Lambs of God*. The evil cult had hatched.

01.29 Hours EDINBURGH HOSPITAL

ANOTHER BLACK RANGE rover pulled into the already rammed full hospital car hospital park. It contained the Brigadier, Dave, and an unnamed man who was sitting in the back seat. They stopped their vehicle behind ours and called Arthurs phone.

"Arthur we are in the car park next to yours." Spoke Dave.

"Roger," Arthur replied to Dave switched off his phone and said to Bash and me, "Come on. It's game time."

We all walked off along the Victorian corridor which had brown / red quarry tiles on the floor. The same colour tile flowed up the wall, but shaped into the skirting board. Then above this were more white tiles with a hundred years' worth of cracking running through them. They finished half way up the wall with a bull nosed green dado tile, and yes, you guessed it, above this is the famous pale blue NHS emulsion.

We were just leaving through the last set of double wooden doors, and we all inhaled our last lung full of Dettol scented air and a century of atmosphere.

We got within five feet of Dave's range rover and the front doors opened. Out climbed both Dave and the Brigadier. No one said anything to anyone at first.

Dave then asked Bash, "Where did you leave the van?"

"At the front of the hospital," Bash replied.

Dave nodded then said, "Let's go. Bash you wait here."

It was a long walk around to the front (*well it felt like it*). The four of us walked up to Ian McPherson in his car he was asleep. Dave tapped on the window with his knuckle. Ian awoke then pressed the electric window down.

"Bloody hell," Ian said.

Dave did not mess about he asked Ian out right, "Ian, how did the cult know where the van would be?"

Ian answered, "What are implying, Dave do you believe…"

Just then the Brigadier butted in, "Sorry Ian, but we need to know how the cult have found out about us. Give me your phone."

"Why?" asked Ian.

The Brigadier then demanded, "Just let me have it, Ian."

Dave moved towards the car. Arthur intercepted him, edging him away. Ian then realising the seriousness of the situation passed the phone to the Brigadier. I just stood there waiting for instruction. Not fully aware of what was actually happening.

The Brigadier started to go through the phone history and messages. Then Ian started his car and shot off nearly knocking over Dave and Arthur. The four of us were just left stood there breathing in the sudden influx of exhaust fumes with the converted gas street lights flickering from dim to semi bright.

I was still just stood there then Dave who was clearly mad said, "Well that's our leak then."

The Brigadier responded with, "I wouldn't have believed it of Ian."

He then lifted up Ian's mobile screen facing us. Lit up in the darkness on the screen was the van registration, date of travel plus motorway M8 sent to an unknown number the message had been deleted. After a silence lasting a few seconds. Dave walked up to the Brigadier and took the phone saying,

"I'll get this to Tanya so she can down load every file off it and get in touch with his phone company find out what has been going on."

Dave pocketed Ian's phone and we all set off back to the range rovers. I thought to myself, if Dave got his hands on Ian then murder would be committed.

Back at the vehicle the brigadier and Bash got in with Arthur. Dave drove off with the unnamed man and I followed driving the van.

02.40 Hours Kavanagh House

SIMON HOWLETT WAS awakened by the high pitched sound of the phone ringing on his bedside table. In response to this, Simon rolled over and stretched out his arm. Then fumbling around on the bed side table, his fingers climbed the brass column in the dark. He successfully switched on the ornate 1920's Tiffany style lamp. He then pulled himself up the bed a bit. Now semi sitting up, he picked up the receiver off the old red telephone.

"Hello," Simon said with a croaky voice.

"Sorry for waking you, Simon." Brigadier spoke.

"Don't give it another thought, Charles," Simon came back with.

"Simon, do you still want to get involved with this operation?" asked Charles.

At that Simon sat fully up and threw his feet onto

the floor, "Too right. I do Charles."

"Do you have a small van or similar sized vehicle?"

"I do Charles. I have a one ton land rover that we use for shooting days."

"Excellent! Can you meet us with the vehicle and a can of petrol at the lay-by just outside the village opposite the fishing pond? And don't...."

Simon cut Charles short and said, "Don't worry. No one will know or follow me. And Charles?"

"Yes Simon?" curiously Charles inquired.

"Thank you." The conversation then ceased and Simon was now fully awake.

He bent over the bed and kissed Annabelle softly on the forehead miming the words, "I love you."

Then left the bed room and walked across the large landing and into his dressing room. He got dressed in his shooting clothes and left the house feeling alive and good. He was now doing something to get his Granddaughter back instead of sat twiddling his thumbs. Twenty minutes later, Simon pulled into the lay-by. There was no street lightning, no moon as he pulled up and parked, dimming the lights. It looked like the second he stopped his mobile rang.

"I'm here, Charles," spoke Simon.

"We know," and two headlights came on and then switched off.

I got out of the van which was parked behind the range rover. Reaching the driver's side of the Range Rover Arthur let down the window. The aroma of strong ground coffee and cigar smoke exited.

"Steve, go over to Simon and ask him to back up to the van so we can empty the equipment into the land rover," said the Brigadier leaning over from the passenger seat.

"Will do Brigadier," I sharply replied. Then I walked over to the long wheel base 1970's land rover, British army kaki green with a canvas back.

Simon opened the top half of the window by sliding it down with his hand and asked, "Who are you?"

"I'm Steve, sir," I replied. I called him sir out of respect for his ex-rank. "Could you reverse your vehicle up to the back of the van then switch off your lights please?"

"Of course," was Simon's reply as he struggled to put the old vehicle into gear.

Within 15 minutes Arthur, Basher and I had transferred all the equipment from the van into the rear of the land rover. The Brigadier was busy filling several rubber condoms with the petrol that Simon had brought. He then tied up six full sheaves and secured them to the ceiling of the van with three in the front and three in the back. The sheaves were tied with string to the rear view mirror. Both the sun visors, the rear ones just looped around the vans ribs through rivet holes. Arthur and I were setting up the night vision goggles we had taken out of the van. The Brigadier was now fixing up a candle in the foot well of the van. Approximately six inches above the wick of the candle was a length of string secured at one end to the passenger chair. The other end was over the rear view mirror and tied to one of the petrol filled condoms.

"You ready, Charles?" asked Arthur.

"Shortly get in the vehicle and ready to go," and the Brigadier then lit the candle. Arthur, Bash and the Brigadier all got into the range rover. Simon got into the vintage land rover with me. The range rover left and I followed. Both vehicles had no lights on as we were navigating with night vision. Which may sound exciting but in reality it's not. Your perceptions of the outside world are two dimensional and the only colour is a bright onyx green with bursts of white. The best way to describe it would be, like you had been beamed inside an early 1980's bad video game.

Five minutes and a mile down the road we pulled over. The Brigadier looked at his watch. Then in the rear view mirrors of both vehicles was an inferno.

The van had burst into flames, "I'm good. Still got it," said the Brigadier.

We had pulled over. If we had been driving using night vision when the flames went up, we would have been blinded. Night goggles amplify the intensity of light times a thousand. Lights on, we took off again and within twenty minutes we were sat in the kitchen at Kavanagh house. Then we got a few hours' sleep.

08.50 Hours

I AWOKE IN a strange very large and comfortable bed in a very nicely decorated and furnished room. You know that feeling you get, when you wake up you don't move for a minute and your brain is trying to locate where you are. Well that was me for about twenty seconds, then to add to my confusion the bedroom door was knocked on once then opened.

I laid there not moving, while a gorgeous seventeen or eighteen year old girl walked up to me in the bed. She gently placed her hand on my shoulder, pushing me softly and said, "Come on sleepy head. They want you down stairs."

I must have then awoken properly. From the second the gorgeous girl removed her hand, everything flashed back into my head. It was as if a USB stick had been plugged directly into my brain. The explosion last night, Ian doing a runner, the operation, and where I was everything came flooding back.

I threw myself out of bed. The girl who was in my room had several bruises on her face, so I took it she was Abbey. I also remembered her photo from the briefing at Dave's. Abbey then looked down and didn't look back up.

I realised I was knackered, and yes, I then stood in that pose shoulders rounded. My hands were cupped over a certain part of my anatomy to if possible prevent any further embarrassment.

Then abbey said, "I'll be off." Just as she got to the door she turned and with a cheeky smile on her face said, "Nice to see *all* of you Steve."

Then the door closed. I grabbed my clothes and rapidly dressed. Exited my room and started to walk down the stairs towards, where I remembered the kitchen was last night. I heard voices getting louder and louder so I homed into the vocals both female and male. Reaching for the door handle, but before I got to it the door opened.

"Ah Steve! There you are. I was just coming to see if you had got lost," commented the Brigadier with a smirk on his well-worn strong face.

The Brigadier went backwards into the kitchen and I entered. Dave had arrived accompanied by the un-named man in the vehicle last night and also Sarah and Tanya were here and stood talking with abbey. Well, I say talking when they saw me all three of them looked in my direction smiling and raising their eyebrows.

Then Sarah on queue said, "Morning big boy." The whole room laughed. Luckily, I was wearing some stubble, so I hope the blushing was not visible.

Dave and the unknown man were talking to Anna-belle and Simon. The Brigadier had a map out on the breakfast table corners held down with the teapot, marmalade and jam pots. He and Arthur were leaning over the map drawing circles on land marks. Then Diana lifted off the teapot, and gestured to me to come and get a cup. This was to the Brigadiers annoyance because the map rolled in on itself. Standing over at the cooker was Ian Mc Pherson. Arthur spotted my reaction as I walked towards Ian.

Arthur jumped in and said, "Not what you think-ing Steve. Last night's show has been sorted out. The connection was from Ian, but not directly! One of the local Bobbies (police) had taken a back hander from a cult member and blue toothed Ian's phone. Tanya found the cloned messages on the server."

Ian then walked to me with his hand out. I shook it but was still not happy. That stupid mistake nearly cost Chris his life. But at least, we didn't have a rat amongst us. He had just made a mistake and left is blue tooth switched on. I guess if you're in the middle of a British police station, you would imagine you were safe.

Ian then went on to say thanks again to Tanya.

I then took Diana up on the offer of that cup of tea and a slice of toast with homemade jam. Everyone then started to leave the kitchen and make for the drawing room which was now our command centre. I supped up then followed, last out and always late that's me.

We were crossing the large hallway when the doorbell rang three times, sounding like a very low toned version of church bells. Diana appeared from the kitchen and walked to the large front door simultaneously drying her hands on her 50's pale blue and yellow piny. Just as she opened the door, Annabelle came out of our command centre making her way graciously across the stone floor to join Diana.

The door wide open, I glanced towards it as entering the CC. Standing there were two men and a woman. The sun was so bright behind them. They appeared like a negative photo, framed by the centuries old large ornate door case. One of the men handed something to Annabelle.

Opening the large envelope, Annabelle swayed and Diana propped her up. I ran to the door to see what was happening. In Annabelle's hands were pictures of

Susannah having sex in some sort of ritual. At the door, I could see the two men who were in the late twenties early thirties. They were dressed in black suits, white shirts, in similar fashion to how the Quakers would dress.

The male who had given the envelope to Annabelle was smirking and offering another envelope. I took this from his hand and passed it to Diana. The man didn't seem too pleased I had done this and leaned forward and attempted to take the letter back from Diana.

Stepping in front of Diana and Annabelle I said, "That's not very polite."

He replied, "Don't interfere or you will get hurt."

I laughed. The man slightly to his left then produced a flick knife and said, "Go away or you will be shaved." (cut)

Smiling at his comment I punched the first guy, knocking him out then exited the door way and invited the gentleman to cut me. By now, Tanya had appeared at the door.

"Careful, Steve," was her comment and then the girl who was with the men started to back off. I saw Tanya go passed me, towards the girl.

She started crying and shouting, "I'm not with them! Don't hurt me. I want to help you."

The man holding the knife glanced her way and growled, "Shut up bitch or you're next!"

By this time the man on the floor was starting to come around, so I kicked him across the face so hard that this splattered his nose and looked like dislodged his jaw bone. This angered the knife wielder and was now childishly throwing the knife hand to hand as if to scare me or impress me.

The knife then stopped in his right hand and he came at me slashing, right to left then back up then right to left again. When the knife went back up right, I moved in grabbed the inside of his hand and wrist. I quickly twisted it outwards. He dropped the weapon and was forced backwards. Then, I rabbit punched him to the throat. He was struggling for breath and clutching at his windpipe and had dropped to his knees, so I kicked him in the face to put him out.

Tanya had hand cuffed the girl and by the time I bent down to pick up the knife Dave, Arthur and the Brigadier were there. Simon had escorted Annabelle back to our CC room.

"Right, let's get the shits inside," said Dave.

Arthur grabbed the feet of one of them and dragged him in the Brigadier asked, "Do you need a hand with the other one?"

"No, sir," I told him as I shoved my hand down the back of his collar and dragged him in that way.

The posh hall now resembled the foyer of a city night club at chucking out time. The young girl was crying and handcuffed to the main stair post, and the two men were out cold lying on the floor. There was blood all over the stone floor. Diane then walked up to me with a cloth and bandage.

"Let me see," she asked in a caring Scottish accent.

Shit it was mainly my blood. The knife had cut the side of my palm, fucking blood everywhere.

All I could think was I hope it wouldn't stain the stone floor. Ian was now on his mobile with Scotland Yard, arranging for these two idiots to be taken to London. They would be charged with assault with a weapon with intent to harm. That should keep them off the streets and out of contact with the cult for the next week at least and that's all we needed. Just then Simon came rushing through from the CC into the hall shouting and then started kicking and punching the two men.

Arthur grabbed him and then the Brigadier got hold of him, "That's enough Simon! That's enough."

"Fucking scum. I'll kill them," shouted Simon.

The reaction was clearly due to him seeing the photos of his granddaughter in perverted sexually explicit pictures. Something no dad or granddad should ever see. It just wasn't right for any parent to see something like that!

Tanya and Sarah had now come through into the hall. The girl was screaming and becoming hysterical. She must have been petrified after watching Simon kick shit out of the two men like an unhinged psychopath.

She was sat on the bottom step screaming and with every muscle fibre in her body, trying to get up to run to escape. This was futile since Tanya had tied the handcuffs to the noel post made of solid oak. She was going nowhere. Sarah approached the girl, placing her hand on the girl's shoulders pressed her down to be seated. Sarah then squatted in front of her so the eye contact was the same level.

"Calm down. Nobody will hurt you," Sarah said as she tried to comfort the girl. The frightened female stopped thrashing about but could not stop sobbing. She was also breathing extremely fast and shallow.

Tanya then appeared from out of the kitchen with a paper bag.

Sarah placed the bag opening over the girl's mouth at the same time saying "Calm down, breath slowly."

The blond girl stared back at Sarah through tearful, petrified sweet eyes. Her long hair which had originally been tied back was now all over the place in her mouth, glued to her face with salted tears. Two large black shapes had appeared under her eyes where the mascara had been dissolved by the sodium.

The paper bag had started to do the trick. She was beginning to breathe slower. Tanya bent down to take off the hand cuffs. This girl was no threat. She was like a rabbit caught in headlights. Paralysed with fear. With the hand cuffs off the rabbit jumped up onto the next step and curled up. Diana fetched a glass of water and gave it to her. Sarah thanked her and held the glass out to the girl after about fifteen seconds Sarah put the glass to the girl's lips and tilted it. She started to swallow then placed her hand on the glass relieving Sarah of the duty.

Ian had now organised the arrest and transport of the two messenger boys who had just delivered the photos. Two officers were being dispatched from Newcastle with instructions to take them to London Scotland Yard. The Brigadier was talking to Dr Thornton who was the mystery man in the car last night, basically saying this unfortunate little set back has inconvenienced the Dr's Speech.

"Not to worry," said Jeremy as he was looking over at the now quiet girl still shaking.

The girl said, "Thank you," as she handed the glass back to Sarah, who was now sitting next to her on the same step. Tanya then gently took hold of the girl's fingers on both hands and turned her wrists. These were in a hell of a mess, cuts, bruised and bleeding from where she had tried in vain to escape the handcuffs and run for her life.

"Steve," Tanya shouted over to me.

"Yep," I turned to reply.

"Take a look at these please." I started to walk over to the three of them sat on the stairs. As I got to within about five feet of them. The girl hunched up again in fear.

"Please don't hurt me. I am on your side. I can explain," she mumbled. Sarah and Tanya both re-assured her that I was just going to take a look at her wrists to see if we could dress them.

The wrists were in bad shape. Three cuts needed stitching and her right wrist could be busted, but at the least twisted.

"What is your name?" I inquired. She did not re-ply, still semi-curled up.

She whispered to Sarah, "Claire."

Sarah replied, "Well done, Claire. Now, please let Steve take a look at your wrists and let's get them dressed for you." The girl nodded and held out her arms in my direction.

Dr Thornton was stood near to me just outside of the CC, half talking to the Brigadier, half listening and observing the girl. "She is in a mess," posed the Brigadier.

"Captive, dominated, abused, confused, a drone... interesting how she broke free to be allowed to come with these two thugs," replied Jeremy. Then he said to the Brigadier. "She could be a decoy."

"What? She must be a good actress then. The state she got herself into," answered the Brigadier.

"She probably does not know she's one, but she could be full of false information (*Their own personal Trojan horse*). Then, allowed the opportunity to abscond in a way where she believes it's all her doing. Remember who we are dealing with Charles," spoke Jeremy.

"Yes, we will need to treat her as a hostile intelligence," answered the Brigadier and they walked back into the CC.

The CC now consisted of two eight foot fold away tables down the left side of the room. These had been butted together to produce one long table, sixteen by three feet. This had a red cloth draped right along it with two chairs behind with a laptop in front of each chair. One printer in the middle and a number of in/out trays up and down the make shift desk.

Running off this at the end like dominos joining was another fold up table draped in the same type of cloth.

Behind another chair were some more trays, but no computer. To the right of the desks were three clear plastic marker boards, four foot tall and three feet wide. One of which, had already photos stuck to it and scribbles all over it in the form of notes. As time ticked on these boards would become our world for the next three days.

Behind the single table stood a large TV monitor with cables running all over the room and make do power points. The concept of a functioning headquarters had been achieved.

Ian and Arthur removed both the delivery boys to a cellar to await their imminent departure. Both had awakened, battered and bruised, but alive. Simon, Annabelle, Dave, Charles and Dr Thornton were all now chatting in the CC. Tanya left the girl with Sarah and Abbey. Tanya was now connecting leads from the lap tops and running other cables with weird looking multi-coloured connectors onto the large TV a hive of activity.

The well under weight pretty blonde girl was now much calmer and sitting at the large breakfast table in Diana's territory. She was wearing one of Abbey's jumpers a big fluffy mohair thing which completely buried her. Abbey then tied back the girl's hair and wiped all the running mascara off so she no longer resembled Alice Cooper! Claire even though now clearly at ease would not let go of Sarah's hand.

Abbey walked away from the table to the large black Agar oven where Diana was making scrambled eggs for their unexpected guest.

"Di look! Look at Claire," asked Abbey.

Diana removed the pan of eggs off the heat and glanced towards the table "Why Abbey!" Diana's mouth fell open.

"I know! She looks like her double now that she's cleaned up," Abbey spoke.

"Amazing grace," loudly said Diana, eggs prepared and peppered. Abbey and Diana returned to the table placing the plate of eggs in front of Claire. Sarah noticed the pair of them looking at Claire.

"Eat up girl. Put some meat on your bones," spoke Diana.

"Thank you," Claire mumbled and then placed the tiniest amount of eggs in her mouth. After half of the plate had been eaten, Claire pushed it away from herself and said, "It was lovely, but I am full." She then looked at Sarah and asked if she could speak freely.

"Of course, Claire," responded Sarah.

Claire then let go of Sarah's hand and placed both of her hands around the mug of tea. Then she glanced over to Diana and Abbey.

She said, "I know why they are looking at me like that."

Sarah asked, "Like what?"

"They think I look like Susannah. Don't you?" Claire proposed.

Abbey and Diana looked at each other and together

said, "We do."

Claire then started, "I'm the same height as her, same measurements or I was a few weeks ago. My hair was done the same as Susannah's, and I even had her little frog tattooed on the inside of my leg the same as her."

"What tattoo?" A puzzled Diana asked.

Abbey said, "It's correct. Right leg inner thigh. I have one the same one."

"But Susannah has a large mole near her kidneys," Diana remarked looking bewildered.

Claire pushed her chair back a bit and stood up. She lifted up the jumper and blouse and showed them her mole. "Basically, I was Susannah's *clone*."

"My God!" was Diana's comment.

"Unreal. It's the same," Abbey said as she shook her head.

Sarah said, "I think we should ask Dave to come in. Will you be ok with that Claire?"

"Yes, if you stay."

"I will," answered Sarah.

Abbey stood up and said, "I will go and get him." Spinning around and she was off. Diana picked up the plate of left over eggs and removed it to the sink.

I think what had just been said was a little bit too much for her to take in straight away.

Abbey now in the CC ran straight up to Dave and said, "Sarah wants you. Umm... Needs you...." She then apologised for interrupting.

"What is happening, Abbey?" Annabelle questioned.

"News, we hope about Susannah," replied Abbey.

Dave started to walk towards the door. Annabelle looked at Simon and they both set off behind Dave.

Dr Thornton shouted them back, "Let Dave go first. If she is willing to talk, it's important we don't overwhelm her. Dave needs to get as much information as possible for the operation to get Susannah back."

The couple waited realizing he was right and remained in the room.

Back in the kitchen, Claire had got hold of Sarah's hand again squeezing it now much tighter than before.

Dave entered and the girl was clearly becoming anxious.

"It's fine Claire... Relax. Dave is just going to talk with you," reassured Sarah.

Dave reached the table and pulled out the chair opposite to where Claire and Sarah were sitting.

Sitting down Dave introduced himself, "Hello, Claire. I'm Dave Sissons, and we are here to help get Susannah back."

Sarah placed her other free hand on top of Claire's and prompted her to tell Dave about what she knew the cult were planning. Claire looked at Sarah then at Dave and started talking.

11.30 hrs

CLAIRE'S FIRST WORDS were, "Dave... sir... if I can help you, will you help me please? I am frightened for my life."

Dave nodded, giving Claire hope. Then, she continued, "I have been with the cult since I was about six years old. When my father died, my mother joined the *Lambs of God* and took me with her. I am originally from Detroit, Michigan in the US. All I remember was my mum coming home from the Church one evening with two men. All our stuff was hastily packed and taken out to an awaiting coach with *Lambs of God* in really big letters on the side. One of the men and my mother had to prise me from my Grandma, who wouldn't let go of me. She was shouting at my mother to re-think what she was doing and to leave the child with her," she took a deep breath, obviously still remembering the moment clearly in her mind.

"When we got on the coach, it was full of other families and everyone seemed happy. Everyone was singing, talking and eating. We seemed to have travelled for a couple of days as it got light and dark again. A few more people got on the coach. Then, I remember, just as it was getting light for the second time, the coach pulled up outside this Ranch with timber houses. There were several different buildings, animals, and lots more people. I remember that they were all wearing the same old fashioned clothing. It reminded me of a movie set.'

'At first our stay the Ranch was good. We even had our own school. Though I do remember that what they were teaching us was a lot different to what I had been learning at my other school. The girl's education stopped when you reached twelve years old, and we were expected to help the women with chores. We then had two classes a week to learn cooking, sewing and child care. The first three years at the Ranch were happy. We made new friends and settled in well suspecting nothing of the ranches true evil under currents.'

'We lived together with another eleven women and fourteen children in a dormitory type building. We were sharing utilities such as toilets and washing. Everyone at the ranch had their meals in a communal dining hall however different people sat at different tables I realised later that this was due to a points system," she said as she cleared her throat. She situated herself in her chair before she continued.

"We had been at the Ranch for just over two years when my Mother had given birth to my baby half-brother. On his second birthday, he was tattooed on his left shoulder with a dot. I know now that this was to indicate that Joseph was a son of Harold Fletchly, *Our Father*. My mother had been selected to be a family mother. That's what they called them, and I know it sounds weird to you but to us it was just part of our life.'

'Harold Fletchly was the only person that anyone could call Father or Pa or any title along the lines. At the age of three these boys were taken from our communal huts, and they then lived in separate dwellings. They were dressed differently and educated, to a very high standard also received tuition in all the arts and ways of the world. Yet still, this vast knowledge given to them would subliminally contain enough false idealization guidance for the boys to become Fletchly's élite and guardians of the cult. The majority of these would become expertise in law, accounting, and medicine. The boys as they were called also had to be treated differently like royalty. It was as if we were all second class to them!"

Claire's body language and demeanour whilst talking about been second class was intense she was right back there in the ranch. She had been speaking for a while now, whilst Sarah and Dave listened in astonishment at this girl's disturbing life.

Sarah then asked Claire, "Would you like to take a break?"

"No, thank you. Please let me continue, I want to tell you everything. I want everyone to know what an evil being Harold Fletchly really is."

At this point Diana brought some cups and a tea pot to the table. Diana then left the kitchen carrying a tray of tea and headed towards to the CC.

Sarah poured three cups of tea, only putting milk and sugar in two of them. She slid over the black tea to Dave.

Claire after taking a drink looked to Sarah and said, Thank you." She placed her cup on the table and started to speak again.

"Two months after my brother Joseph had been taken away from us. One of the other women who lived in our hut had reported my mother to the *dark men*. This woman told them that my mother used abusive language against the Father. My mother had only asked, 'Why does he have to bloody take our children?' That evening, my mother was taken from our hut and brought back several hours later. They just dropped her like a jelly fish out of water. She was covered in human faeces and all her hair had been shaven off. I ran to my mother only to find that she was unconscious. Her face was covered with cuts and her nose had been broken in more than one place. All of the other women helped me get her to the ablutions room, where I washed and tended her wounds. My mother never walked or spoke again. She died in bed two months after that night from septicaemia. There was no funeral as the Father had condemned my mum's soul. She was soulless according to him and her body was fed to the pigs," Claire said as the tears streamed down her face. Dave looked down to the ground; his hatred for Fletchly had now risen to a new level.

She took another deep breath and continued, "The dark men were like police on the ranch, and everyone was encouraged and even rewarded for informing on others rewards were anything from extra food, time off your chores, shopping trips out of the ranch and ultimately sex privileges. There were no intimate sexual or emotional relationships allowed in the ranch community. To ensure that no one strayed from the rules, attractive and sexually aged females were forced to put on this pungent body smelling odour derived from pig manure and urine. Sex was given as a reward by the Father. Any sexual act been committed without permission... including masturbation, would be severely punished. To the point of castration for males and in the female cases, they were often never seen again.'

'I later found out later that they would end up in the dungeons and were used as sex toys for Fletchly's boys. Or they were used in the cult's prostitution rings all over the world. It was also a known fact, but never talked about that. Some of these unfortunate females were tortured, then murdered by Fletchly. He followed this with Necrophilia sex with their corpse!"

Claire at this moment was emotionally unable to carry on telling her plight, the frightened creature was uncontrollably sobbing. She then wiped the tears away with the back of her hand and with some resilience looked straight at Dave. It was clear to him at that point this girl had some fight in her and the horrendous life she had to endure up to now would have broken most people. Dave at that moment didn't say anything to Claire, but he knew she was telling the truth. He would ensure that she would receive the same help as Susannah and she would have a chance of a decent life. Even if he had to pay for it himself.

Claire removed her hand from Sarah's and sat up a bit then continued, "Three days after my mother's body had been decimated by the animals, I was put into a locked room no bigger than a dog kennel. I couldn't stand and couldn't lay down. There was no natural light, and every hour approximately a light came on for ten minutes. When I was first thrown in the dungeon, I could mentally work out the days, but as time passed by, day and night became one. Two tin plates of gruel and a tin of water were given to me through a small trap door at sporadic intervals.'

'Running along the back wall of the dungeon was a six inch gutter where you went to the bathroom. Every so often, some water would wash this away and depending on how much water came through, you often ended up with other people's excrement. Whilst in the dungeon I had my first period. I was so frightened I had not been told about them by anyone really, but I actually thought I was going to die. I was in there for a long, long time. I had lots of periods, then out of nowhere I remember hearing male voices shouting, '*Where is she? I thought she was dead. Let her out! I want my daughter.*'

"Then my dungeon door creaked open. Standing there silhouetted by the corridor light were two men one of them was the Father *Fletchly*. He had a blanket open in his hands, '*Come to me my child*'. I couldn't move even if I had wanted to. The man with him crouched down and came in to my home to get me. Bending down, the man picked me up and carried me out.'

'Then Fletchly wrapped the blanket around me. Then carried me out of the building my eyes had to be covered. They placed me into the back of a van. I truly don't know to this day how long I was in that dungeon." She stopped talking for a brief moment and looked over to Sarah. By the expression on her face, you could tell that this was hard for her to talk about. She looked down to her hands in her lap before continued talking.

"My finger nails had grown at least two inches and even curled under. My hair was right down my back and my breast had developed... I had developed in other ways as well. I'd transformed from a girl into a woman.'

'The van transported us to a very nice house. It was a large and well-furnished, wooden plantation style home. We couldn't have been that far from the ranch, as we only drove about ten or fifteen minutes. Once inside I was handed over to two black ladies dressed in uniforms decorated with white frilly aprons. They both helped me up the stairs and into a large bedroom with a free standing bath in the centre of the room. The bath was drawn and full of bubbles. I was stripped of what rags I had left stuck to me as most of my clothes had rotted away.'

'Once in the bath, I was washed and pampered by these two maids, but they never spoke. About an hour had passed and another maid entered the room. She placed fresh towels on the bed with some clean underwear and pyjamas with a dressing gown. The maids were towelling me down and putting creams on me. I had developed a lot of sores whilst in the dungeon. I think they were all sores, but sometimes I was awakened by rats gnawing on my flesh. I asked the maids what their names were but they didn't answer.'

'*Why won't you speak?*' I raised my voice slightly. Both the Maids then looked at me and in unison opened their mouths. Their tongues had been cut out. All that was left were small lumps where the tongue had been severed." Claire at that point raised her eye to Sarah again, in an attempt to seek comfort.

"Eight months had passed and I had been treated like a Princess by everybody including the Father. Then one night around seven p.m. my two maids, now my friends, came into my room. I knew their names to be Juliet and Betsy. The three of us had developed our own touch language as they were both illiterate.'

This night however instead of them been in high spirits, both of them looked glum and didn't want to look me straight in the eyes. They drew the bath and bathed me as normal; this may sound arrogant on my part but I was not allowed to wash myself, do anything for myself really, like I said treated like a princess. But still in total fear of the Father. Then got me dressed in new exotic lingerie. Did my hair and makeup very different from my normal plain style. This was as if I was entering some beauty pageant."

Claire brought her hands up to her face as if she were ashamed to continue. Her words were spoken softly as she continued, "At 9 p.m. the Father entered my room. He told me that tonight was my special night, and it was time for me to prove I truly loved him. This man was a monster. At 10.15 p.m., I was raped in every way imaginable, bleeding from every intrusion. I was made to perform oral sex for hours while he forced himself down my throat making me constantly gag. I actually threw up twice, which I believe gave Fletchly more pleasure.'

'The digital alarm clock flashed 02.32 a.m., and I was curled up crying on the now blood, vomit, and semen stained sheets. I was unable to move not only through the pain I was in, but also my fear of him. I laid there feeling my personality about to fragment in order to save my sanity."

Sarah moved closer to Claire at this point and put her arm around her. "Fletchly at one point when I had tried to refuse oral sex, had got mad and torn of the cable from the bed side light. He whipped my bum with it until it bled. I at this moment actually wished myself back in the dungeon. The following day after what Fletchly called my blessing, he came to my room with Juliet and Betsy and another man in a suit who I had never seen before.

He told me to stand and then informed me that the opportunity had come for me to be of great service to the *Lambs of God*. He ordered the maids to remove my clothes and lay me on the bed.'

'I was so frightened I became frigid. I thought this other man was going to do what Fletchly had done last night, but thankfully he didn't. He put his brief case on the bed near my feet. He opened it up and put A4 sized photos on the bed of a blond girl taken close up from all angles. The girl in the pictures I now know to be your Susannah. The man then started to measure all my body parts. He drew lines with a felt tip pen under and around my breasts, my thighs and some on my face. After then taking photos of me. He walked back to Fletchly and was pointing to me and at the same time pointing to the digital image of me on the camera. He was nodding and looking. Then, Fletchly smiled and patted him on the back. After this the man packed up his stuff into his case and was escorted out by Juliet. Fletchly approached me as I lay on the bed. I locked my legs tightly shut and my hands were protecting my private area.'

'He leaned over and kissed me on the forehead then stood up and said, '*You will be a great asset to us Susannah*'. I looked puzzled then he spoke again, '*That is the name you are now known by.*' I could see the fear in Betsy's eyes as he walked by her. He cruelly stopped and shouted '*BOO*' at Betsy. She tensed ridged with pure fear, and after a few seconds you could see the urine coming out of the bottom of her long black uniform.'

'Fletchly now out of the room. I jumped up and off the bed, ran to the bathroom and grabbed a towel, running back to help Betsy. She was still frozen to the spot. Her eyelids were so full of tears like dams, ready to burst. After placing the towel at the bottom of dress to soak up her urine. I hugged Betsy tight and whispered to her that I loved her.

At this point Sarah butted interrupted her by saying, "You should be very proud of yourself for coming through all that and then being able to tell us and ask for help."

Claire nodded before she continued, "Throughout the following year I had lessons on how to walk like Susannah, behave and even think like her. And whilst all this was going on in the United States, Susannah was being groomed by the Cult in Edinburgh, England. Six months ago, I was flown into Scotland and was assigned a language specialist. She was to teach me to now sound like Susannah. The final stage was for me to be Scottish and Posh. I had undergone at least six plastic surgery procedures, before I arrived in your country. This physically had made me into Susannah. When I was then introduced to Susannah, and we both were told that I was a double for her. My role was to help her with the mass of duties she would have to carry out as the Cults' new ambassador. Susannah and I became friends… good friends. She is such a lovely person, but has been lured into the Cults belief system fully. Just like my mum was a life time ago."

Claire squeezed Sarah's hand. She finished the last drops of her tea, and then said, "I am here because I could not let another human being go through what I went through."

Dave asked, "What do you mean by that?"

Claire answered with her revealing words, "One night a couple of months ago, Fletchly visited my bedroom again. I felt powerless as he abused me. When he finished degrading me for his gratification, his mobile phone rang and he answered. He walked away from me a bit, but I could still hear him. He was going on about Susannah being taken to the Ranch and thrown into one of the dungeons. The same one I had been in. He was also saying that once Susannah signed over the Kavanagh Estate, and the grandparents had been evicted. The cult would move in their ancestry home and this puppet pretending to be Susannah would be the link to the aristocratic society of England. I made my mind up then that I could not save myself but I could prevent Susannah entering into my world. This might sound silly and pathetic, but I felt so worthless and beyond help. Not worthy. But saving Susannah gave me a purpose."

Dave then apologized in advance for his forthcoming question. "So Claire, if you're such an important part to Fletchly's plan, how come you turned up with them two idiots who are clearly delivery boys?"

Claire replied, "They were taking me to the Doctors. Part of the Father's plan was to start having me replace Susannah. He wanted me to get known as her with these every day important agencies. I got out of the car when the door opened and I ran behind them. I was going to beg to use your toilet to get in but then the violence started."

Dave said, "We will help you Claire I promise that, but you must understand that for this next coming week… we will have to keep you here."

Claire replied, "Thank you! Thank you!" and she through her arms around Sarah. Reiterating that she would help in any way she could to save Susannah.

16.00 Hours BRADFORD

CHANG AND MARLEY had been busy setting up the conservatory for another briefing. At the same time arriving were twelve of Dave's other employees they began pulling up at the front of the mini mansion. They entered the building in two's and one's carrying military style Bergen's and black holdalls.

They all dropped their luggage in the hallway and Chang showed them through to the conservatory, where the chairs had been set out in two rows facing a large monitor. Gary walked up to Chang and Marley who had prepared sandwiches for the briefing and asked where Dave was?

Chang replied, "There has been a delay in Ireland, so the briefing will be remote from there."

The ten men and two ladies were chatting amongst themselves, laughing and catching up with each other. The conservatories triple glazed glass ceiling and walls were amplifying their voices, translating them into humming tunes and throwing the melody back into the mix of blurred conversations.

The majority of the group were now choosing sandwiches. Joanne, one of the ladies had just put her cup under the Massimo coffee machine, then pressed 'Mocha'. She was just tearing tops of a couple of packets of brown sugar when George appeared next to her.

"How are you, Joanne," asked George as he passed her a slim version of a lolly stick to stir her drink with.

"I'm great George. I have just got back from Afghanistan been working in the field hospitals." Joanne was a combat nurse as well as a CPO.

George then asked if she knew what this operation was about.

"No," Joanne replied. Apart from the length and time plus that she and Julie the other female were doing medic duties on this opp, specifically the long distance transport of a sedated P/T.

"Can everybody take a seat now, please?" asked Chang.

There was a bit of a rush for coffees, then a couple of minutes later the chairs were shuffled about and filled. Chang was plugging a cable into the phone which connected it to a conference speaker phone with four speakers. (A spider)

The monitor started flickering and pictures were appearing then freezing. A couple of the lads started singing '*Why are we waiting…*' Gary and George got up to help Chang and he allowed them to take over and slowly just moved away, realising that he was out of his depth with all this technical stuff.

Just then, you could hear Dave's voice loud and clear then Gary asked George to re-do the two scat leads. He did so and they had images of Dave and the others in the command centre. The voice was slightly out of sync. Dave's mouth moving a split second before the words were heard but it was acceptable.

"Evening all!" announced Dave as he was looking to see if all twelve had arrived.

"Glad you could make it. Joanne, hope we didn't

cause too many problems for you."

"No Dave. But tired though. Flew into RAF Brisenorton this morning," answered Joanne.

One of the others then asked Dave where he was.

"You know better than to ask that, matey" replied Dave. "At the end of this briefing you will all be fully instructed on what you're doing but not where or when."

Dave then continued, "Because of the nature of the people that we are up against on this one, we have brought on board a specialist in this field and are very lucky to have him with us here. He has agreed to deliver a lecture to us on the subject of *Religious Cults*. I will now introduce you all to Dr Thornton."

On the screen now you could see Dave moving from and Jeremy coming up to the lectern. When the words religious cult had been mentioned, this caused a little stir in the conservatory. The crew had started asking each other if they had known about this cult and what cult? Another was saying '*Nutters, Freaks*. This will be fun.'

The Doctor was now already standing behind the clear Perspex lectern with a few pieces of paper resting next to a remote, plus a glass of whisky with a few cubes of ice. The Doctor had started to speak, yet nothing was heard in the conservatory just visuals. Tanya then appeared on the screen clipping a mike onto Jeremy. He gave a small laugh and said thank you to Tanya.

Slightly flustered and apologising the Doc started

again squaring of his papers by tapping them on the lectern and a quick crafty wet of malt. (*Dutch courage*)

"Thank you for being patient everybody during my little cock up and thank you again to Tanya for helping." Then nodded towards where Tanya was sitting in acknowledgement. "I could talk for a week on this subject, but I believe Dave has allowed me an hour," Dr Thornton then started.

The Doc had been talking for around twenty minutes covering other cults and had just finished informing every one of the exploits of the people's temple. This resulted in over one thousand people or followers to move to a so called paradise utopia. After only nine months the leader, Jones shot a visiting American member of congress? The result of this was a mass suicide of men, women and children, nine hundred sixty-five people dead. Whilst Jeremy continued with the lecture, there was a knock on the door and Diana opened it invited two men into the hall, after they had given their names and produced there warrant cards. She then knocked on the Command Centre door.

"The Police are here Brigadier," announced Diana.

Ian and Arthur got up and went into the Hall. I think Arthur to be fair had not wanted to hear any more of the lecture. He had gained his knowledge of cults a different way to the Doctor.

Outside of the command centre, Ian produced his identification for the two officers both plain clothes. They passed over some papers to him which he read then folded, nodded and handed back to the detective.

"Follow us then gentlemen," Arthur said on the turn. All four set of turned towards the cellar.

Back in the Command Centre, Jeremy said that he had just been explaining the new ideas around thoughts on Stockholm syndrome with relevance to people been kidnapped and abused. He said that they would stay with these abusers, tormentors, defending them. The rationalisation of why these relationships were happening to the point of recruitment of others. (*It was getting fucking deep*) The term Stockholm syndrome is usually tossed around in the field of kidnapping. It was first introduced by a professor after a bank robber had taken hostages in 1973. Sweden and the hostages subsequently sided with the hostage taker. Jeremy had spent time dissecting the available data regards Stockholm and patterned this with similarities of cult behaviour in relation to follows been abused and remaining in the Cult.

Jeremy began to explain his main philosophy of what made cults tick. He took his time to explain, "To be successful is not down to some magical form of brain washing. It was the ability of the charismatic leaders of all these cults to implement idealistic views of the individual's image of their own version of utopia. To do this successfully the narcissistic leader will use every tool in his psychological box." He looked out to the crowd, checking for our understanding. He then looked back at his notes before he continued.

"Just like any large successful marketing company,

these Cults sell and portray an image to be part of… to fit in or to be one of a community. It is human nature for eight out of ten people to need a pat on the back… to have the need to fit in. The product is really irrelevant. It's what the brand physiologically or emotionally gives you or you take from it. Humans will be willing to follow. They will believe others over themselves. They will not question to the point of committing atrocities. So let's say a successful cult creates the perfect front for its organisation." (*Their shop front.*)

"The first people you meet will be usually new to the cult, fresh faced and full of genuine excitement about their new organisation. They passionately believe that they have discovered something, and that they now belong to or fit in. They have been accepted, so they now belong. Neurologically, they start to be happy and this tells their brain to produce dopamine, one of the most potent and addictive chemicals that exists.'

'Dopamine is the brains chemical that persuades our bodies to fall in love. (*And we all know how addictive that can be*) So artificially the cult begins to drip feed us this drug. The clever deception arrives when people start attending meetings. Nobody gets put in a trance or hypnotised, and they don't walk around transformed into a zombie. Gradually, the willing participant who would usually be at a low point or vulnerable time in their life, subconsciously looking for a way out of his/her present mundane, sad not full filling reality.'

'At these meetings the participant is welcomed, invited in. They feel unique, wanted, and special (grooming). A few more meetings and the willing participant has become a follower. Initially the religious aspect is possibly of no consequence but over time without realising the cult has started to feed you subliminal messages. The next phase really depends on the cult and how far they take their disciples.

If the cult decides that they want you to become part of their 'family'. You will be invited to seminars, retreats and told that there are only for believers. You are one of them after a number of these. You are *in* as you believe. You have taken the first foot on the ladder, and you become a willing party to what you are informed is privileged information. Which will usually be made up bollocks. At this point, you have most likely been to see the leader speak, and you are captivated and let's not forget flattered.'

'You are now in more and at this point being as-sessed in secret. They will vet you both as an individual, and financially the results of this will determine the future phases you go through. If they decide they want you in and living/ working in one of their communes, they will ensure that through prolonged exposure to the belief system that they have already bombarded you with and that you have not rejected. They will deprive you for weeks of lengthy sleep, ensuring that throughout days and nights you will always be involved in some mindless task, which they inform you is important.'

'You will have no time to think freely, no access to your old life. You will be of course still have free will, however at this point your free will be focused on successfully completing this phase. You're in as you're a chosen one remember… you now *Belong!*'

'They have decided you are ready to become symbolic to them. You see yourself now as part of them and you have actually controlled your own mind. Yet you still allowed yourself to buy into their product or beliefs through inclusion of a hierarchal cult type belief system, which you are now part of. Rather than any external brain washing the catalyst of your mind control has been from the start the cult's belief system satisfying you beliefs.

'Free will, although cherished by western countries, is very hard to define and a lot of scientist and philosophers dispute whether free will genuinely exists. Because if humans are to be swayed and choices are given, arguments are put forward. We choose a way, path, direction and a cause to belong.'

'So to sum up what I hope has not been too boring for you all, Cults always have a single narcissistic charismatic leader with his own set of beliefs which he aims to ensure become your beliefs. Through inclusions, introductions, psychological, and emotional catalyst, you change your own free will. Or at least what you believe is your own free will."

Jeremy then finished his whisky and just stood there. Then the Doc walked back to his seat next to Tanya, there was a quiet applause yet meaningful both in the Command Centre and the conservatory.

"Take a 15 minute break then I will continue," spoke Dave to both rooms.

The two officers entered the cellar behind Arthur and Ian. The two cult delivery boys were sat back to back with their arms and torsos tied together with rope. In the dim lighting of the cellar. The two captives looked pitiful... bruised, battered and unable to move with their mouths taped up.

Arthur walked up to the men and started to untie the yards of rope. The officers had come behind Arthur with their hand cuffs out, and the two cult delivery boys were re-secured. The men were then bundled into the back of a VW black van. The van sped away, while Ian and Arthur made their way back to the Command Centre. Just as Dave had returned to the lectern,

Arthur put his thumb up and nodded to Dave. Dave acknowledged Arthurs removal of the two thugs, by raising his eye brows and giving a slight nod.

Then Dave said to all, "Can we start again please? We have a lot to get through and time is ticking."

Then as the troops in the conservatory poured back into their seats. Tanya was summoned to the lectern by Dave who was struggling to get the projector working. Tanya then pointed to the lap top and informed Dave that the power point files had to be open. (*As if telling him off*)

Tanya tapped the lap top screen three times, "Try it now, Dave."

"Thank you, Tanya," said Dave as several bullet points appeared on the screen.

Dave then spoke for twenty or thirty minutes, covering all the basics of the operation. His final words to the gang were, "From 22.00 hrs today people, you will need to be ready and on standby for a one hour window. Our standby period's duration for this opp is to be seven days. Any questions?" Dave asked. No-one replied.

The conservatory screen went blank, and Chang switched on the lights. Most of the team made their way back to the coffee table. George made his way to Chang and shook Chang's hand. With a slight bow, he asked Chang for the accommodation keys. Chang passed him a large piece of wood with a key, tied to hit. Chang also gave George a piece of paper with six digits on. George turned to the group and waved the wood. He then left the house via the rear doors.

———————

Back at Kavanagh House 23.40 hours

SIMON, ARTHUR AND I were in the kitchen. Arthur was just putting camouflage on Simon's eye lids with green and black cam cream. When he finished, I turned off the lights, and we waited a further fifteen minutes in the dark before we exited. We made our way to the road approximate ¼ mile up from the main estate gates.

Basher left the house 30 minutes earlier in the vintage land rover. It was all a ploy for any eyes watching the estate. We had been sitting in the edge row for around ten minutes when Basher screeched the land rover to a halt, just in front of a field entrance.

The night had become darker, damp, cold, and the Scottish wind made sure we were very aware of the conditions as it invaded every layer of clothing we were wearing. The old tarmac road ran a couple of metres past the edge where we were hiding the surface was shining in places. The moon light reflected of the patches of decade leaves which had been pasted to its surface by the local farm vehicles relentlessly rolling from field to field. Bash got out of the vehicle. Leaving the door open, he walked in front of the land rover and then kneeling down as if he had hit something. He glanced back to the vehicle and whilst gazing into the beams of light, he found himself counting the dozens of moths and insects. It seems were caught in this space age tractor beam.

He then got back up and pretended to kick some object into the hedge returning back to the vehicle. He reversed the vintage wagon into the field entrance and remained there for twenty-five seconds. Bash switched off the lights, and we jumped into the back.

With the lights back on, we drove off. Thirty or so minutes later, we had driven a distance of twenty-two Scottish miles and exited the tent on wheels.

"See you, Bash," I said as I tapped him on the shoulder.

"Yes, God speed, to you all" said Bash, and we slipped down the bank of a ditch. Then we started to crawl along the water filled bottom. I was in front, followed by Simon, and the rear brought up by Arthur.

The ditch been approximately six feet deep gave us perfect cover from any prying eyes. We ran through the eighteen inches of water, rudely awakening the native wild life. Sliding our feet through as if we were skiing to keep the noise low. While we were ploughing our way ahead, Simon had fallen, even dived on several occasions. Then he was picked up by Arthur. I will give him his due though, as he didn't whine once he got up and soldiered on. He was more than double my age and his motivation to help his granddaughter more than likely numbed any pain.

Once we were out of the ditch, we spent forty minutes patrolling the area. We had stealthily got ourselves into position within a small wooded area. It couldn't have been better. The trees and vegetation growth was surrounding an old dried up pond. Arthur crawled to within a foot of a wire fence always keeping at least a foot inside the cover line. He was totally concealed, started to focus his night specs on the cults dwelling.

Within an hour, we had set up an operational observation point. This would now be manned permanently 24/7 until the operation ended.

The time now was approaching 03.30 hours, and the rain had decided to christen our new home. It pissed it down, but at least we had gotten our bevy up giving us some cover.

We were actually quite dry but chilly. At 04.30

hours, the rain had given up and eased right off, so Simon crawled to Arthur with a plastic green case. They set up the laser identification scope, which is a brilliant piece of kit. LIS as we called her once she had been set up. We could at a distance of three kilometres produce a 3-D drawing of any object, from a rabbit hutch to a stately home. The only drawback of LIS was it had to be used on a clear day and in daylight. It resembled a large old fashioned video camera on a tripod. You sighted the LIS and then with a remote you drew dots around the object of which you desired an image. Then you had to follow a sequence of instructions on the screen.

Depending on the size and details involved, the LIS would within a time line of thirty minutes to eight hours produced a 3-D plan of the exterior, then by entering the architectural information, etc. The LIS produced drawings of the interior so on this operation this information would be priceless.

"Simon, can you go and see if Steve has finished setting up the sensors for the perimeter? Tell him it's time to start back to get picked up," whispered Arthur.

Simon crawling backwards replied, "Sure, Arthur."

Simon looking knackered returned to the centre of our new OP. I was sitting next to the bivy, connecting all the cables for the buzz lines and testing the four inch monitor. I had placed three cameras out to cover the OP's rear and flanks. Simon passed on Arthur's instructions to me then had a mouthful of water from his plastic bottle.

"Are you alright Sir?" I asked Simon as he lowered is black water bottle.

"Yes… Yes, I am thanks Steve. Call me Simon please. It's been a long time since I was a sir," Simon finished talking and he just stared into space for a moment, reminiscing most likely,

He was soaked but his cortex barber jacket was repelling most of the water. He had his plastic hood up over his head, pulled tight around his face with a draw string secured with a toggle under his chin. Water was dripping off his nose, lips and eye brows. The hood was one of them which you unzipped from the collar pulling it out as you needed it.

I crawled up to Arthur and left him the monitor for the cameras and also gave him the flask of coffee.

"See you tonight," I spoke quietly.

04.40 Hours

SIMON AND I were leaving the OP. Let's just say that dawn was up and drinking his coffee. We had thirty minutes before it was fully awake, and it would be light.

Waiting for us in the vehicle would be Bash.

07.35 hours EDINBURGH AIRPORT

THE BRIGADIER, DAVE and Tanya all walked through the already opened doors. Both the Brigadier and Tanya were in uniform. Dave was wearing a made to measure suit, with a Mac style coat, which was drooped over his arm. Dave and the Brigadier were carrying a black leather holdall, and Tanya was pulling behind her a small case on wheels with a handle protruding out from it.

To say that the clock had not yet struck 8 a.m., the airport was buzzing. There were passengers queuing at booking in desks ten deep. The shops and food outlets (*McDonald's and Burger King*) were dispensing coffee from all over the globe. People taking it like their regular medicine.

Police Officers were walking around in pairs with nine millimetre sub-machine guns strapped to their bodies. Pilots and cabin crew were crossing paths, and cleaners were removing yesterday's grime again as tomorrow never comes.

Tanya veered off from the other two and presented herself to the British Airways coordinator for business class. He then took the tickets from Tanya as she checked and scanned their tickets. All three tickets given back to Tanya, he informed her with a cheesy smile.

"Flight A6670 departing from Gate 62 in twenty-four minutes."

Taking hold of the tickets again Tanya said, "Thank you," and walked off with them still in her hand.

The camp airline coordinator who was manning the business class check in desk stood as if he was holding a pound coin between his arse cheeks.

Now in the departure lounge, Dave placed his coat over a chair and his holdall on it. The Brigadier sat opposite with his holdall between his legs. Tanya still pulling her case walked straight up to the massive frameless panes of glass and stood staring at the dozens of planes taxing around the runway.

After a few minutes Tanya turned and looked directly at Charles who was thumbing with his mobile. Tanya still gazing, headed towards him.

Charles looked up in Tanya's direction and said, "Are you sure you have not lost your passion for planes?"

"I have not, sir." fired back Tanya. Charles smiled and looked towards Tanya with proud father like eyes.

Tanya then asked, "Do you remember when I first flew into this country with Chang and Marley? And you were here to greet me just like you promised."

"How could I ever forget that Tia." They were both smiling now and locked together in a memory only they shared.

Butting in Dave asked, "Do you want these drinks?"

They were all flying to Amsterdam for the final briefing with the other nations involved with operation 'Take Down.' Along with the Brigadier, Dave and Tanya would also be there. A very Senior British Cabinet Minister was present (no names mentioned) and the final decision to then go ahead with the operation would be down to him and his counter parts from the other countries. The brigadier, Dave, and Tanya were there to answer any questions and convince any sceptics that this operation was feasible and ready to be executed. (*And between me and you the hardest job these three would be to convince the politicians of all nations that this would not come back on them and ruin their careers.)*

This meeting was not only tactical, but part sales as the combined cost of the operation would be into the millions.

For all these countries to fund the *Take Down* of Fletchly and his disciples. It had to be a success both practically and politically. But let's not forget that each country was also in for a share of Fletchly's fortune. I'm not saying that this had any persuading factor!

Twelve hours later and the meeting was over and now the waiting game began.

19.40 Hours

CHARLES, TANYA AND Dave were walking from the Airplane shuttle bus and into the VIP area back at Edinburgh Airport. Dave stopped and looked at his phone which was vibrating and lighting up with the Minister's code name appearing on the screen. (Caroline office)

"Hello, Sir," answered Dave. Then he listened.

"Thank you very much, Sir," he replied after a short conversation, which ended in a call me as soon as it's over.

Tanya who had noticed Dave had stopped, watched him put his phone back in his pocket, and then half punched the air.

"Oh Dave?" Tanya asked moving quickly towards him Dave put his thumbs up.

He then said to Tanya, "Do the honours."

Tanya rang Chang and instructed him to mobilize the team. On putting the phone down Chang went to the conservatory and pressed a large dome shaped green button located next to the light switch.

The minute he pressed, it he saw through the window that the building next to the weapons range had lit up both internally and externally. Chang went to the kitchen and switched on two kettles plus he put a couple of pans of water on the gas rings to poach eggs. Within twenty minutes the crew was assembling in the kitchen.

"What's the plan, Chang" asked George as he bit into an egg sarnie.

Chang replied, "Finish drinks and sandwiches then helicopter."

"Helicopter?" asked George.

"Yes, a couple of Wessex will be landing in fifteen minutes and taking off again in thirty minutes.

KAVANAH HOUSE 20.40 HOURS

ARTHUR CAME RUSHING into the Command Centre, his hair still wet/ damp and in need of a shave. However, he was forgiven as he had only been back from the OP half an hour previous, and the photos and Intel he had captured were first class. It would give us the entry team a fantastic advantage.

The Command Centre's desks were now not so bare, and Sarah sat behind one of them was shuffling bits of paper as if it was a competitive sport. The

Perspex free-standing boards were now a gallery for all the photos and technical drawings of the targets.

Arthur had also managed to get some really good close up photos of the *Hit*, Fletchly, with the zoom lens.

LIS never let us down. It did us proud. The technical drawings that the machines produced were practically architecture blue prints.

Sarah also had been busy, and with help from Claire. We now believed the room which contained Susannah was on second floor. It was at the end of a long corridor leading to a separate annexe, which was Fletchly's domain.

Still, this information would be treated as hostile intelligence, because the source was not vetted. (*Believed to be genuine, but people win Oscars for acting*).

Dave now stood in front of the Perspex boards. The only people absent from this meeting were Abbey, Diana and Annabelle. Simon attended as he would be occupying the OP with Bash. However, Bash would not be looking through binoculars as his job was to prevent any of the HIT list leaving the building. Out of us all, Bash was by far the best shot and with Simon there to spot for him no Jackal's should escape. The briefing was kept short. We all knew our tasks and roles.

Dave asked, "Any questions?" No-one said anything.

The electricity had started to flow. Arthur put his arm around my shoulder, urging me to walk with him, just about to cross the threshold of the Command Centre and out into the hall.

Tanya shouted, "Be careful Steve! And you too, Arthur."

Bash and Simon were already dressed in full combats and ready to leave in the vintage land rover. The Brigadier, I think was just pepping them up with the, '*Officer to Lads*' talk. (*Ha ha, but funny enough they do work*). WOW, just out of the blue my adrenalin switch was clicked.

01.15 Hours

Resembling two swat team members, Arthur and I got out of one of the range rovers. Both of us in full black combats with black fleece hats, and faces camouflaged up. Dave was also out of the range rover, now ensuring we were carrying out our final checks.

There are about ten jobs to do. A ritual maybe, but also made you realise you were going to war! I felt like a new recruit again going through basic training, jumping up and down to make sure nothing rattled or broke loose. I checked Arthur's face, and he returned the favour. These may sound silly little things, but they are so essential. Just then, we all heard the unmistaken sound of the Wessex coming in. The Brigadier opened the door of his Range rover. This meant all four of us now were standing on the retired runway of the old RAF Glochlon airfield.

Dave then pulled what looked like bike lights out from his pocket and walked twenty yards away from us towards the centre of the concrete runway. He switched the lights on and placed them on the floor. Both lights were as powerful as light houses giving off a burst every two seconds. The lights would only last five minutes, but this would be enough for the wocker wocker to spot us land.

Dave returned to where we were standing, and then Arthur and the Brigadier simultaneously pointed into the dark starless night. There revealed was the flashing amber and red beacons of the Wessex. The body still not visible, cloaked by the dark night and Scottish mists.

The pulsating lights descending on us like some ET taxi. Hovering twenty feet off the ground, and we were virtually blown away. The down draft was awesome. Silly, I know. Just big boys and bloody big boys. (*But one of these machines landing within feet of you was as if the laws of physics had been rewrote.*)

The door slid open, and the helicopter crew member was hanging out of it. They were looking below to ensure safe landing of his passenger bus. He was wearing smooth light kaki green overalls and a green helmet with a mike bent around from the side of his helmet to his mouth. This allowed him to communicate to pilots via a piece of sponge.

Landing lights time had now expired. Their powerful beam of red light ceased totally, remaining activities were illuminated by the Wessex's beacons. The RAF crew man had his small search light fixed just inside the door. In the cab of the helicopter now visible were the pilot and co-pilot carrying out their end of flight procedures. Dozens of switches been flicked off. Also you could just make out the pilots lips moving as he spoke into his round bit of sponge attached to the helmet mike.

He, at this point, would have been given instructions and confirming to the second Wessex that they were down. Then playing from the sky was a treble beat of rota blades (*no other sound like it*). At this point, the bird on the ground lit up again as if it was a male animal carrying out a mating ritual to attract his mate.

The now second bird was making its decent. Landing thirty feet in front of the first Wessex. The second helicopter was carrying George, Gary, the two girls, Joanne and Julie, (*as the ambulance had now been delivered to this base*) plus two other members of the team. This helicopter had been fitted out with ambulance equipment. George was first off the bird, jumped off whilst it still hovered to the annoyance of the RAF crew man. Bird on the ground, George helped the girls off, purely as a courteous gesture as these two females could hold their own as good as the men. George releasing his hands from the waist of Julie as her feet placed squarely on the old concrete.

(*Good set of lads, these RAF helicopter crews. I remember once in Ireland. It was, I believe, our first flight in a helibus and cruising approximately at 1000 feet. The pilot announced we were having engine problems. Fuck me, can you imagine what we were all thinking. Then the engines stopped and the bird fell fast out of the sky. Ten seconds later engines going again, and the pilot spoke over the headset,* 'Welcome to Ireland' *ha ha.*)

Now on the ground, the rest of the six team members were jumping out still hanging around the doors as the RAF man passed them their gear. The propellers slowed and majestically came to a stop. Gary then walked with the girls to join the rest of the team. George made his way over to Dave and the Brigadier, who were now talking with the Pilot of the first Wessex.

George on approaching Dave made a salute gesture to the Brigadier.

He replied, "Thank you, George. How are you keeping?"

"I'm fine, Sir. Thank you," George answered and then addressed Dave with information about the team.

"We are all here Dave and equipment is been checked now. What are our orders?"

Dave reached into the back of the Range rover and retrieved a plastic beaker handed it to George then grabbed the flask.

By now the Scottish mist which had already engulfed the first helicopter was hovering towards the second. Dave opened the tin flask and poured George a full cup of coffee. The aroma from the fresh ground coffee kissed George who then took a sip. Dave then handed George a piece of paper with instructions regards the transport for four men in each Range Rover. The two girls were waiting for a van to arrive which would be used as an ambulance. The remaining

2 men would be staying on the air field for security.

George then had a bit of chit chat with Dave and the Brigadier. Finished his strong black coffee, handing back the mug to Dave.

"Cheers, Dave. I will get this lot sorted and ready to move out."

George walked away. Dave was putting the cup away, when Brigadier asked, "Is there was any coffee left?"

47.5 miles away in the Cults Cave

HAROLD FLETCHLY WAS cutting the teenagers pants off with an antique scallop. It was long and sharp with a thin blade and ivory handle. Whilst the girl was being tied and strapped to a torture table, one of the helpers told the girl to stop screaming. She did not stop, so the same sadistic helper punched her in the face. Then, he shoved a horse bit in her mouth.

Now secured down and unable to scream, the second helper dressed in a medieval looking monk robe, bowled over a distressed wooden table full of old surgical instruments. Fletchly's eyes were clearly widened as his hands felt and explored the torture tools. This equipment that used to save lives was about to snuff one.

The teenage girl, now violently being penetrated by the first helper, was in pure hell. This innocent young girl was reared on the ranch from the age of six. She was then asked to come and meet the Farther today to be christened. She was excited and full of joy not even been able to imagine the sadistic acts that were about to be committed to her.

Fletchly then told the helper to stop and get out of his way. He then sinisterly put a curved six inch knife in front of to the victim to increase her fear, before proceeding to cut an oblong shape of skin off the girl's thigh. This sick act caused the petrified innocent girl to pass out. Fletchly had cut and removed a skin graft large enough to put over the girls mouth.

He then removed the horse bit and proceeded to glue and stitch in place this piece of perfect skin. He dismissed the helpers. They left Fletchly in the dungeon with his play thing. The two people one man and one woman removed their monk robes and hung them up, just inside the dungeon doorway.

The woman exited first and the man slammed and locked the door behind him. They then together walked through the lavish Jacobean room and into the corridor.

The woman had then only taken twelve steps when a young girl of approximately ten years old ran up to her shouting, "Sally, Sally look, look come and see the flowers." Dragging Sally by the hand, they left.

RAF RUNWAY SCOTLAND

ARTHUR AND I were talking to the pilot of the second helicopter discussing our entrance into the Cults lire. The two of us were to be dropped on the roof of Forester's Lodge by the Wessex.

We would then break free off our harness's and

quickly enter the building via the roof. After we showed the pilot photographs of the building, the pilot was then able to assess the drop from his perspective.

The pair of us started to slip on our abseiling gear and test the equipment. Julie then came over and jokingly started to take the piss out of us. You would know why if you had seen someone in a harness, not a good look on a male.

"Very fetching," said Julie.

Arthur replied, "Steady Julie. Don't flirt with Steve, or you will have Tanya to deal with."

I then said to Arthur. "Leave it, mate."

Arthur said laughing, "It's clear to everyone you two should be together."

"Fuck off," I snarled.

Julie then approached me saying, "Good on you mate. She's lovely and if you do get together, look after her. She's one in a million."

I said nothing as I got a healthy well done slap on the shoulder from Julie who was now telling Joanne about the up and coming romance. Arthur was sat on the Wessex smirking.

The night although dark and misty was warm now as the wind had dropped the mist held in the heat like nature's own quilt.

Joanne announced she had brought pack up.

"You hungry lads?"

"What you got?" half shouted Arthur.

"Marley sent you prawn noodles."

"Steve, you have a choice of spring rolls or egg and

cress sandwiches."

"Sandwiches please," I said quietly.

Joanne said, "Don't be shy about Tanya, Steve. She is like our little sister."

I just smiled slightly with embarrassment, then ate the sandwiches given and supped my tea. (*Big beast tamed*).

Julie then asked the pilots if they would like something to eat.

"No thanks, we ate before we came but a drink would be welcome." A flask and 3 cups were passed their way as Julie was discussing the weather with me.

Joanne asked Arthur, "What time is zero hour?"

Arthur replied looking at his watch, "Ninety minutes away. We take off at 03.00 hrs."

Joanne replied, "Thanks Arthur. We will shoot off in the ambulance at 02.30 hours." The two girls then retreated to the ambulance to carry out final checks.

02.15 Hours

THE TWO RANGE Rovers quickly entered the grounds of the Kavanagh estate through the rear gates. One mile from the main house, they were driving with no lights of any kind, navigating with in the two dimensional world of night vision.

The black vogues screeched to a halt ten metres from the rear of the kitchen door. All eight doors simultaneously opening. Annabelle whom had watched the vehicle's arriving opened the rear kitchen door and exited to greet them. It was a formidable sight she witnessed. Ten men all easily towering past six feet and not one under fifteen stone. They were dressed in black combat overalls and carrying weapons, faces blacked.

Now, for the first time since this escapade began, Annabelle believed seeing these mercenaries that she would soon have Susannah home.

"Annabelle, my dear," said the Brigadier as he got up to her.

"Charles, you look twenty years younger." Annabelle replied.

He chuckled as he replied, "Flattery will get you everywhere." Somehow he also knew to give her a hug and as he did this he whispered, "I *will* bring her back."

Choked up with tears Annabelle kissed Charles on the cheek and said, "I have not stopped loving you… ever."

Charles just pushed away slightly from her, keeping his large weathered hands on her shoulders and smiled.

Dave then approached the pair of them, Annabelle still with tear filled eyes just said, "Thank you for all this."

Dave replied, "Don't you give us a second thought. This is just another day at the office for us, Annabelle."

Then the remaining ten of the team walked passed Annabelle one at a time making the gesture of tipping their hat and saying in rough deep male voices

"Morning, Ma'am."

Annabelle felt like royalty inspecting the guard, and her tears dispersed in their place came joy and confidence.

Diana, as requested, had laid out several layers of old sheets on her kitchen table for protection. Because as the lads came in the kitchen, they placed their weapons on the sheets and started to strip them down. As they cleaned them, both the Brigadier and Dave began handing out rounds and stun grenades. The atmosphere of the Kitchen was one of excited warriors

George then shouted, "Fifteen minutes lads!"

Weapons started to reassemble and when completed the only noise in the room to be heard was the cocking of weapons.

The testosterone began to pump vigorously through the men. Each soldier of fortune was lined up and inspected by the Brigadier, with Dave walking behind him. Just like the army, regardless of whom you were… What you were. On an operation like this, you were a team member that was the only way you were coming back.

02.50 Hours

ON THE RUNWAY, the Wessex had woken up and started to move its blades. Arthur and I jumped on board as the blades were now rotating that fast they appeared as one.

The crew man slid the door shut and announced to the Pilot, "Good to go."

He then received back, "Roger that!"

The pilot then engaging the engines fully, which broke the laws of logic and lifted this two tonne machine into the air?

At four hundred feet the helicopter burred left in flight, and it would take eight minutes to reach drop zone doing one hundred and twenty miles an hour.

Four minutes passed and the crew man leaned in towards Arthur and me, putting four fingers up to inform us that we had four minutes left. He grabbed my harness hook tugging it and pointed to the door which he then started to slide open. Arthur and I both knew he wanted us to get attached to the drop lines. The noise now was deafening inside the bird. There was a combination of colossal sounds, each one deafening on its own. Yet somehow, the orchestra of blades, wind, rain and engines created beautiful music.

The crew man then received another message from the co-pilot, "Two minutes to drop and launch in one minute."

"Roger that."

The crew man again turned to Arthur and me, putting up one finger. Then sliding his hand across his own throat which indicated get ready, both shuffling across the checker plated aluminium floor to the open door. Sitting on the side of the helicopter, I lifted up a D shaped coupling ring which was inserted into the floor. I clipped mine and Arthur's drop ropes to the ring then tugged on them.

I looked at Arthur and laughed as his cheeks were blown about in the wind. Arthur then lifted up his hand to me offering a High 5. The Wessex now starting its turn and slowing down to thirty miles an hour to drop its pay load. We both through our abseil ropes out then a tap on the shoulder. Down... we slid twenty-five feet to the end of the rope.

Flying through the air, I could see the lights of the black Range Rovers skidding to a Holt in front of the Target building. The helicopter started to circle the building again, coming around for the third time. This was it as now below resembled a Guy Falk's party... the stun grenades, flares, and thunder flashers. They all started exploding. I saw the entrance team blowing out the ground floor windows.

With a *Bang,* Arthur and I hit the roof at twenty to thirty miles an hour. Arthur instantly snapped off his harness rope.

I however was being dragged up the roof smashing tiles with my shoulder as my harness clip didn't release. Thank fuck for the crew man been observant he had seen this and he severed the rope at the Helicopter.

Just at this point, amongst all the chaos and fighting, Dave shot up a red flare which was the signal to enter the building for me or Arthur. On the roof, Arthur was looking at my shoulder, my jacket was ripped around the shoulder and clearly some amount damaged had occurred because there was blood.

"How does it feel?" questioned Arthur.

I started to rotate my arm in a circular motion showing my partner I was ok. Thumbs up and nodding from Arthur. Then the two of us quickly smashed a hole in the old roof tiles. We sawed through the wood tiles and dropped into the void.

Now in the loft space, we unslung our weapons

and cocked them. I, whilst spanning my weight between the roof trusses, pocked a small hole through the plastered ceiling. Arthur then slid through a small fibre optic cable connected to a two inch screen.

Arthur announced, "On target. That's the hall or corridor, and it's clear."

I now had a Stanley knife in my hand and was slicing the plaster board along the roof trusses. I managed to cut a couple of feet oblong. Arthur switched of his torch. The last thing he saw was me tucking my elbows into my sides, and my machine gun flat to my chest. Then, I jumped a couple of inches in to the air legs brought together. I went straight through the pre-cut ceiling and hit the floor. Instantly, I para-rolled forward and was upright in a blink of an eye. I began stalking the corridor with my weapon shouldered, not even a second passed when Arthur was down and up against the wall

Whilst I ensured the corridor was kept clear, Arthur was on his hands and knees pocking his fibre optic lens under the first of six doors that opened into the hall.

The hall/ corridor had no natural light and the luxury of fresh air wasn't present. It smelt like a well soiled residential home. Decade's old carpet which resembled a rockabillies' greased hair. Pictures on the walls were the cheapest possible, imitations of all known masterpieces including the Mona Lisa. All the doors, skirting boards, architraves were original at least ten coats of paint smothered on everything visible to the eye.

All rooms were cleared barring one. For the sixth time, Arthur opened the door. He kicked twice and the door flung open. I came rolling into the room and was presented with a group of five women and two children all huddled together on one 1950's metal framed bed. The stench was even greater in this room, due to the fact there were four ablution buckets overflowing next to the wall.

After clearing the rest of the room, I turned to the door way, nodding to Arthur and started to exit. Arthur began to walk away from the door way, I had gotten three or four feet from the door when one of the women dived and grabbed my leg wrapping herself around it. Then, I heard the sound of five shots. Unable to shake the bitch off my leg, I spun the top of my body around and smacked the woman in the head with my rifle butt. Running into the corridor my heart turned to lead. I saw Arthur on the floor with blood being pumped out of his neck.

At the bottom of the corridor thirty foot in distance was stood Fletchly. I had stupidly let down my warrior guard and was now about to being executed. Fletchly just stood there. My brain was processing everything around at immeasurable speed. It then came to the conclusion Fletchly was out of ammo. When I started to lift my weapon, Fletchly ran. I dropped down to Arthur and placed my hands on his jugular, the pressure of the pumping blood was so great, the thick red fluid was still penetrated past my fingers.

I then heard footsteps running towards me, instantly

thinking Fletchly, I grabbed my pistol and looked up.

It was George, "Come on Steve. We have got Susannah and this place has been rigged to blow."

I told George to get the women and the kids out of the room. They went running off down the corridor. I rapidly dressed Arthur's bullet holes as best as I could. I shoved a dressing on his neck and rapped two rolls of surgical tape around it, just so I could just move him. George then helped me pick him up and throw him over my shoulder. We both knew not many would have stayed like this, but I refused to leave him.

I then shouted at George, "Run! Run get the fuck out. I'm following you! Run George."

Carrying my new partner, I ran the length of the grotty corridor knocking the imitation pictures as I fled. My left shoulder smacked into the wall as I turned to descend the flights of stairs. Bouncing down each step I struggled to keep Arthur on my shoulder. My arm was tight around his thighs, but his head and upper torso were rocking and moving across my back. As I reached the bottom step, my leg nearly gave away. It was if I was standing on a rolling bottle. Looking up, I sighted the last few people exiting the main doors. Stopping for a split second to secure Arthur, I was off again. Ten metres across this hall, and we would be out and safe. Standing at the main door, encouraging me to run was George and Gary. It looked like they were going to come in and help so I waved them back. Dave then appeared and pulled both of them physically away. The look on his face was one of gloom. I was within feet of the main door. I saw everyone outside then…………..

WHITE LIGHT EXPLOSION…………..

6 HOURS LATER KAVANAGH HOUSE; DEBRIEFING

ARTHUR AND I had been taken to hospital. Susannah was already in France, travelling in an international ambulance. She had to be sectioned and also sedated during her journey through to the retreat in south of France.

Dave then handed over to the Brigadier, "Thank you all for attending. Not good news all-round, as you will already know. We have four in hospital. Two critical, however, we did succeed on retrieving the package that we went in for. I can also pass on to you all now that the rest of the operation *Take Down* across Europe was very successful. And, the Americans have informed us that the ranch was taken with minimal force."

Charles sipped his drink, then Tanya popped up to the lectern and handed him some sheets of paper, "Thank you, Tanya," politely said the Brigadier.

He then continued "Also, we can confirm that the cult's assets were all frozen." Shaking the papers Tanya had just given him. "And this means Fletchly may be *Evil Walking*, but he has no major funds. We have a chance to get him and the two remaining targets as two have been removed." The Brigadier then sat down next to Dave while John took a turn at the lectern.

"Hi, all. Let me start by saying glad to see you all here and let me apologise for my lack of attendance on this operation. I'm sure you will all know that I would have loved to have been there, but I had other stuff to attend to. Right, down to why I am here today. I'm sure you are all aware by now of the fact that on this operation, we have been cursed with a leak of information."

At this comment there was movement and talking in the audience. Listening, John let them vent a few minutes. What he had just said would have been like swallowing a fucking large pill with a vile taste.

"Thank you for your concern,"

Then Gary put his hand semi up and said, "John is that why we got Susannah so quickly? Because the cult was literally moving her out?"

"Yes," John said.

Another of the crew shouted, "Who's the fucking mole?"

John came back with, "Now. Now. Let's calm down. We are looking into this,"

The Brigadier gave John a look. "What I would like is for any one that believes they might know something regards the leak to get in touch with me or Tanya. Let me just say that Ian was not at all involved with the leak."

The briefing continued for another thirty-six minutes, then Dave thanked and dismissed every one. Tanya made her way with Sarah to Edinburgh hospital.

EVIL WALKING

Stephen Lewis www.clonedforreward.co.uk

Evil walking, the next book in this exciting series. The hunt for Fletchly from Stephen Lewis. The story becomes more intriguing with twists that will lure you in then! When you think you have got on the trail, it twists again. Follow the characters that you have warmed to and work with them to capture the personalities you now hate!

Made in the USA
Charleston, SC
16 June 2015